JOURNEY IN HEAVEN

Bob Northey

Northcott Publishing

"The moment we take our last breath on earth, we take our first in heaven."

Dr. Billy Graham

CONTENTS

MY ARRIVAL

A thick, swirling cloud wraps itself around me like a dark shroud. There's nothing to see or hear - just murkiness and an eerie silence. Beneath my bare feet, progress seems strangely slow on the smooth, well-trodden track. I'm alone. I've no backpack, money or mobile phone.

'Where am I? How did I get here? Where am I going?' Questions bombard my mind and I'm struggling to find answers. The weird thing is, I don't feel anxious.

'Could this be just a dream?'

A faint fragrance hangs on the humid air. I breathe in deeply and banish my solemn thoughts. Beyond the fog, I imagine an English apple orchard in full blossom. A warm feeling of hope begins to settle on my muddled mind. I start to pace myself, and with each stride I clench both hands, and stretch out my fingers.

'This is no dream,' I tell myself, 'I feel fully alert. I just need to find out where I am.'

The veil of mist begins to thin, and I emerge from the shadowy gloom to discover I'm not the only one here after all. In the dim light I begin to see the silhouettes of other people, who are all walking in much the same direction. With some surprise, I realise everyone seems to be dressed in identical clothing. We're all wearing knee-length, linen robes with loose sleeves to our elbows and soft belts tied around our waists. No one speaks or even whispers, there's just the soft sound of feet gently shuffling at a steady, purposeful pace along the endless, flat paving.

'Why is this place so strangely quiet?' I ask myself.

I start to get really curious. As my eyes re-focus, I begin to glance around at the others and I can't help noticing how different everyone looks. Although dressed in similar robes, the variety of faces suggests that my fellow travellers come from different nations. Many people look middle-aged, but there are a few young adults like myself. There are also some youths and even some little children. Just in front of me I notice a couple walking hand in hand. A very young boy is being carried on the man's arm. The child clings on with tiny arms wrapped around the neck of the man, who appears to be his dad.

All of us are making our way towards a bright light that's now visible on the horizon. My feeling of hope gives way to a measure of optimism, as if the light itself offers reassurance and a sense that everything will be okay.

It's really hard to get the attention of others because nearly everyone gazes forward; no one ever looks back. Once or twice, someone alongside looks my way and offers a brief nod, as if to acknowledge me. I smile back in return, knowing we share the same unusual journey.

Like an unexpected clap of thunder, the truth suddenly hits me and instantly, I realise where I am.

'Heaven! I'm about to enter heaven!'

The truth resonates through my whole being. My emotions explode. A feeling of elation begins to flood my inner self, and the transformation feels amazing. I wonder if anyone else around me realises where they are. I try to shout it out, but no sound comes from my mouth.

This is surreal. My mind is in turmoil. I'm so overwhelmed by the enormity of the revelation that it's impossible to fully process the information. But my mood has radically changed from its earlier uncertainty to a feeling of euphoria and extreme anticipation.

Heaven, I think to myself. Wow, I'm actually stepping into eternity with all these other people.

As I press forward with fresh confidence, new questions start to race through my mind about what lies ahead.

'What will heaven be like? When will I meet Jesus? Will I recognise anyone? What happens when I arrive?'

It's a massive relief to realise I am heading into heaven, and not stuck in some sort of limbo or worse. But it's the thought of meeting Jesus, my Saviour, face to face, that overwhelms me. I feel excited, nervous and almost afraid.

'What should I say to him? How will I feel in his presence? What he will say to me?' I'm searching for answers.

I try hard to imagine what God will look like, seated on his throne and surrounded by his angels. But it's impossible. I have no idea of what awaits me.

The moment of realisation about heaven has jolted my memory, and the reality of my past is rapidly returning.

I was just twenty-seven years of age when I was diagnosed with cancer. Little did I know at the time, I'd less than two years left to live my life on earth. My career as a young architect was abruptly put on hold. Life became a full-on battle as the disease spread, requiring endless visits to hospital for treatment. The loving concern of my family and church meant everything to me. Those final days, spent in the compassionate care of the Sobell House Hospice, are now all but forgotten. The goodbyes have been said to a wonderful family; Mum and Dad, my young brother and older sisters. I've left behind my lovely girlfriend, Catherine and so many great friends and work colleagues.

Before my illness, I hadn't given much thought to what some people called the after-life; even though I'd been a Christian for more than ten years. I'd assumed there would be plenty of time to get ready for eternity, when I was much older and probably retired. My understanding of heaven was very limited; to be honest it was more of a vague hope than a certainty. Even in my local church there was little talk about eternal things, such as heaven or angels.

When things did get bad for me, it took all my effort to cope from day to day. As I lay in bed, I sometimes wondered about heaven but had no real time to think about it. The pastor of my church talked a bit about heaven, when he visited me during my final days in the hospice. Death had come, as it comes to everyone, except for some it seems to arrive so early.

The mist has all gone and I stare at what lies ahead.

'Wow, just look at that!' I say to myself.

In the far distance, beyond the thousands of people walking in front of me, I can clearly make out a walled city, towering high. It's illuminated with brilliant light and the cloudless sky above is tinged with orange and red. Everyone around me is increasingly bathed in the same glowing light, causing our faces and clothing to shine.

Something else is happening and I feel as if I'm being transformed. I'm leaving behind the limitations of the life I've lived on earth, and I'm being prepared for a new future in heaven. It reminds me of the moments a butterfly waits with anticipation to emerge from its chrysalis, before stretching out its wings for the very first time.

Behind me was a life where nothing lasted for ever, and where time was precious. Months and years had passed by very quickly. I'm now entering a realm that never ends, an eternal kingdom where I expect to live constantly in the presence of God among other believers.

I notice a young woman nearby with ringlets of fair hair resting loosely on her shoulders; she looks about sixteen years old. Her pale face is serene, as she keeps her eyes fixed on the sight of the city ahead. She walks with poise and maturity. For a moment I wonder if she feels lonely, as she walks among so many strangers. But I'm quickly reassured by her radiance and sense of peace.

As we make our final approach to the city, I start to hear the first sounds. Not far away there are trumpet fanfares and many voices singing and cheering. Around me the crowd is gathering much closer together. The pace is quickening and the tread of footsteps is now like an army marching to its destination.

I pause, for a moment, to look up at the polished shine of the city's dark red walls. The massive rectangular blocks have been laid in interlocking rows and tower above me some thirty metres high. These enormous walls seem to stretch for miles to the left and to the right.

'It's jasper,' I announce confidently to myself.

I recognise jasper as the prized, red-speckled gemstone used to build the city walls. My dad's hobby was jewellery-making and from an early age he taught me to identify many kinds of gemstones, by their colour, shape, transparency and mineral hardness. The lustre of the walls creates a spectacular array of colour that dazzles me, as it reflects the light of the city.

Above us, hundreds of shining, white-robed angels are providing a heavenly escort. They fly silently towards the city, in formations of between twenty and fifty. Rising high in the sky, they swoop down and criss-cross over our heads. Surprisingly, their presence brings comfort rather than alarm.

Where are their wings? I wonder, as I watch them more closely. They have none and I think, odd, I assumed all angels had wings.

I'm amazed to see some of the angels are holding tiny babies firmly in their arms. These precious little ones are wrapped in small, white linen cloths. Not one of them makes as much as a murmur.

A male voice chorus rings out from a huge throng of angels, seen high above the walls. The blended voices of tenor, baritone and bass, echo all around as the angelic choir repeat their phrases again and again.

'Hallelujah to the King of kings... Amen to the Lord of lords... The Lord reigns on high for ever.'

Another majestic fanfare reverberates above us, with long harmonic blasts and rapid fire notes; all in perfect timing. I count at least fifty angelic trumpeters lined side by side along the parapet of the wall and directly over the entrance. Long golden trumpets are raised high and held to their lips. Above them, the choir of angels stays poised, ready to sing its next anthem of praise.

In front of me, two massive pearlescent gates stand wide open. They measure at least ten metres high. Each beautiful gate is made from a single veneer of Mother of Pearl, reflecting a myriad of glistening colours. Over the entrance is a massive crystal headstone, which carries an inscription. The metre-high capital letters, carved into the red crystal, are inlaid with gold and spell out ISSACHAR GATE. The double-gate is built on a stunning, turquoise foundation of amazonite, which glows with a soft, sea-green effect. At the top of the carved steps, in front of the gates, stands a tall, manly angel positioned like a sentinel. This mighty, shining figure has broad wings that are spread out behind him, and he's dressed in a dazzling, white robe. In his right hand he holds up a long, flaming sword; his glowing eyes are fixed straight ahead. He remains motionless.

It's a tense moment as we begin to climb the set of twelve broad steps, which lead up to the majestic entrance. I feel a great sense of anticipation about this significant event.

'Heaven, here I come!' I say to myself as a feeling of joy begins to rise within me.

Just as I pass the angel guard at the top of the steps, I notice another inscription etched into the sea-green crystal beneath my feet. This one reads PHILIP, APOSTLE. It occurs to me there must be more entrances to the city, which are named after the other apostles. I think about the global impact of those first twelve disciples of Jesus, who opened up the way to heaven through the proclamation of the Gospel. We pass the splendour of the gate, and walk for several metres under the rose-red illumination of the archway. I enter the city of heaven.

It's ablaze with light like no other city I've ever seen. Suddenly I'm filled with unimaginable joy. I can hardly contain it. I try to take in the magnitude of the sight that greets me. Just inside the city gates, on either side of the golden street, are tiered terraces filled with tens of thousands of onlookers. My throat chokes with emotion and tears roll freely down my face.

I'm almost deafened by the loud cheering, which erupts from every side. Moving forward I hear constant shouts of welcome, and cries of praise expressed in many languages. Through my tears, I see that the people waving are dressed just like us in white linen robes. Many of them are also wearing golden crowns on their heads. Every face is turned towards the unending procession as they scan the new arrivals for sight of friends and family members.

Mothers look with anticipation for their children and husbands search lovingly for their wives. Pastors are ready to greet their church members and evangelists eagerly wait to welcome souls saved. Many of the welcoming witnesses quickly make their way down the nearest steps, to greet the arrivals they recognise. This is a welcome beyond my wildest dreams.

As the sound of the angelic anthem above blends with the cheering crowds, I pause to look more closely at the glowing faces of the men and women watching us. I feel sure that among this great company are many heroes of faith. People like Noah, Abraham and Sarah, Moses and Miriam, David, Ruth, Jeremiah, Peter, James, Mary, John and Paul.

But more than these famous names, I know without a doubt, Jesus my Saviour and Lord is waiting to welcome me. Jesus, the forerunner has opened up the gates of heaven, and the gift of eternal life has been secured. Very soon I will meet him face to face.

It's staggering to realise there's been one continuous procession of people into heaven ever since that historic time. Each one of us has escaped the brief grip of death, while our mortal bodies have been left for dust, until the Day of Resurrection. Millions of believers have already entered this eternal city and every single hour thousands more arrive.

Just beyond the grandstands is a large open square filled with several hundred people. Many of the new arrivals are being welcomed by friends and loved ones. They gather in twos and threes on the bright gold paving. Everyone seems to be smiling; there are tears of joy and plenty of hugs and kisses. As I continue to make my way through the crowds I feel elated to be in heaven, but I know the reality is still sinking in.

Up ahead, a group of angels stand facing us and waving their hands. Angels are quite easy to recognise with their shining robes and pure white hair. They direct us to make our way to one of the welcome booths, which are located at the end of the tiered stands. I follow their guidance and walk towards a row of arched recesses set into the wall. New arrivals are talking to angels who are standing just inside each booth. It all looks so busy, but then I spot a vacant space and quickly make my way across to speak with the angel.

'Welcome to Heaven,' says the friendly angel.

These are the first words spoken to me since I arrived.

'You're in Assembly Square.' he says.

The angel pauses, tilts his head slightly and looks over my shoulder as his eyes brighten.

'Your guide's coming,' he says quickly.

Even before I can turn around, I hear a voice calling my name.

'Jamie, it's so good to see you.'

I spin round to see a tall, shining figure of a man with white, wavy hair, which reaches to his broad shoulders. He rests a firm hand on my shoulder for a brief moment and his handsome face beams with radiance.

'Welcome to heaven, my name's Thaniel,' he says in a gentle, warm voice, which sounds vaguely familiar.

As we start to walk out of the square he says, 'You may not know this, Jamie, but I've been watching over your life on earth, and keeping you safe, ever since you were a small child. I've now been sent to welcome you and to show you around heaven, there's so much for you to discover.'

I try to take this in. Meeting an angel face to face for the first time is quite daunting, but Thaniel is no ordinary angel - he's my guardian angel. He must know so much about me and my life on earth; now he's here to be my guide.

'Good to meet you, Thaniel,' I mumble, not quite sure what else to say.

This is incredible, I think to myself.

'There's much for you to see, so let's be going,' says Thaniel, as he nudges my arm and starts to walk on.

Thaniel and I set off together along the main highway, which leads away from the Issachar Gate. I'm feeling rather glad he looks fairly normal, and slightly relieved he doesn't have any large wings. That angel guard looked a bit too scary!

We join scores of other arrivals, many of whom are accompanied by their own angel guides. I begin to get my first good look at this immense city. The main highway is paved with solid gold setts. There are millions of them, laid down like cobble-stones in beautiful symmetric designs forming combinations of arcs, circles and crosses.

I'm dazzled by the intensity of the light all around me and the profusion of colour is awesome. I try to identify the different colours and shades, some look familiar and others I've never seen before. It seems as if everything is bathed in bright, luminous colours of blue, green, turquoise and gold. The brilliance of the light shines everywhere and there are no dark places to be found. The whole of heaven almost shimmers with light, creating a spectacle beyond belief.

From just inside the great wall of the city, there is row after row of beautiful buildings, on both sides of the highway. I lose count of just how many rows there are. The buildings are constructed from highly polished, sea-green amazonite that glistens in the light. Each mansion block stands three or four stories high; most of the buildings have flat roofs with overhanging eaves and arched windows on each floor. Angels are everywhere; some are looking out of windows, others are walking around, or just sitting down in the grassy gardens, which are set out between each row.

Thaniel points to the buildings and says, 'You're looking at the angels' quarters and they extend right around the edge of the city. We angels are kept very busy serving God, but we do get some time to catch up with our friends and neighbours. When you entered the city you would have seen one of the angel guards. These are known as the cherubim, they are a special kind of angel and their role is to defend the city and the throne. It reminds us all of the spiritual conflict that still rages outside of heaven. There's a cherub positioned at each of the city's gates. They used to also protect the entrance to the Garden of Eden, before the great flood was sent across the earth. The cherubim, along with the seraphim, and the four 'living ones', are the only groups of angels that have wings.'

I reply, 'That's very interesting because I was really puzzled to see angels able to fly without wings.'

In the distance behind us, I can still hear the angels singing and the repeated welcome fanfares. I picture the scene in my mind as the steady stream of new arrivals enters the city.

It's just the start of my journey in heaven and it's great to have Thaniel as my personal guide. I'm so excited about what I've already experienced, and I can't wait to make more discoveries. Thaniel explains to me that the City of God is incredibly big.

He says, 'The apostle John recorded the city's dimensions during his visionary journey in heaven. He described the New Jerusalem as a vast walled city, which measured fifteen hundred miles wide from east to west and fifteen hundred miles long from north to south.'

Thaniel continues, 'There's plenty of room to accommodate more than three billion citizens and a similar number of angels have always resided here. The city was created by God, and the people who live in the kingdom of heaven are called citizens. It was designed and built with unparalleled beauty, using pure gold and a unique selection of precious gemstones.'

I ask Thaniel, 'Did I enter the city by the main entrance?'

He replies, 'Not really, because altogether there are twelve gates that lead into this enormous city. Each one is named after a family tribe of Israel. You arrived at the Issachar Gate, which is the middle of three gates built on the south side of the city.'

My guide explains, 'The foundations of the gates at every entrance are built using one of twelve different gemstones; these are memorials to the twelve apostles of the church. The gates themselves are named after the family tribes of Israel. This golden highway, we are walking along, is known as Issachar Street. It's named after the gate you entered and leads all the way to the city centre.'

'Thanks Thaniel,' I reply.

I try to visualise the massive scale of the city, with its twelve gates and main highways that lead to the city centre.

Our journey continues, and we leave behind the high-density, crystal buildings and reach the countryside. There's mile after mile of open space, gentle rolling hills with small woodlands and grassy parks. Walking along Issachar Street we pass through several towns and villages.

Every so often I catch the sound of singing nearby. At one village, we stop briefly in the square to listen to some children, who are singing in two-part harmony. Their young voices are filled with a calm sweetness, as they lift up their hearts with joy.

I smile to myself as I notice more angels flying overhead. They appear like heavenly commuters travelling between their residential quarters and the city centre. What a strong sense of mission they display.

Arriving at another road junction, there's a surprise waiting for me.

'Wow, what a beautiful canal,' I call out.

I hurry over to the edge of the highway and peer down over the bridge into the water. My eyes are dazzled by the reflection of blue sapphire, from which the walls and bed of the canal have been carved.

'This canal is absolutely stunning,' I tell Thaniel, as he joins me.

He explains, 'You'll see more of these beautiful, blue canals as we travel further into the city. They really are so attractive and make an ideal place to take a stroll or even go for a jog. The canals have a constant supply of pure water that's always sweet to taste.'

I ask myself, 'How is it possible to be in a totally new place and yet feel so much at peace?

Already I'm getting on well with Thaniel. There's a wonderful spirit of joy and freedom in the atmosphere and I get the feeling that I really do belong here. Heaven is now my new home. I know that I have family members who were believers and I'm looking forward to meeting them; especially my paternal grandparents.

We pass more countryside and then I begin to see many taller buildings in the far distance. Finally, we leave Issachar Street and turn left along an avenue; this one's called Rachel Avenue. The avenue has its own pretty canal, and leads into one of the many residential neighbourhoods.

A group of three, cheerful-looking angels are sat in front of about a hundred young children. We pause to watch as they share in the laughter and conversation. Every question the children ask of the angels gets answered, and each reply seems to be fully understood. The smiles and surprised looks on their infant faces say it all.

'Almost there,' Thaniel says to me.

Moments later, he stops in front of one of the many beautifully decorated buildings. The outside walls are made from small blocks of turquoise crystal. Large green emeralds decorate the arched entrance with each facet reflecting a different shade of colour. The elegant property looks like a luxury mansion.

We stroll together through the archway and into a small courtyard garden with its own sparkling fountain. There's an abundance of shrubs and flowers in bloom and several groups of people are sitting around on carved, crystal benches. As we pass by, the citizens look toward us with friendly interest and smiles. Then I follow Thaniel up a short flight of steps and along a corridor. Entering through a small doorway we reach the lounge of a large open-plan apartment.

Thaniel turns to me and says, 'Everything is ready for you, Jamie. This is your very own place. You can come and go here whenever you want. I need to leave you now, but you'll see me again soon.'

Without another word, Thaniel leaves the apartment and I'm left on my own. There's light everywhere; the luminous walls are back-lit with restful blues and greens; even the floor is made of crystal that looks like opaque glass.

'This looks amazing,' I say to myself.

The comfortable white sofas and low-level crystal tables make this the perfect place for me to meet up with friends, or simply to relax on my own. I really like the contemporary design and well-lit space. There's even a small writing desk with paper and pens. Sketching maybe? On the two exterior walls the room has floor-to-ceiling windows, which overlook much of the city. I walk across and step out on the small veranda, only to be captivated by the magnificent views to the far horizon. Angels continue to fly through the air, sometimes slowly and at other times travelling at the speed of shooting stars.

I stand for ages, gazing out at the incredible beauty of everything before me. There are so many wonderful buildings, each with its own unique colour and design. As expected, most of the buildings are designed for personal accommodation. But I'm astonished by the size and sheer variety of the other buildings spread across the city centre; it's way beyond anything I ever imagined.

Heaven is a busy place, but for all the activity the only sounds I hear are the distant echoes of music and the occasional cheering crowds.

I'm about to leave my room, when I see two figures standing at the door. I look at their faces and suddenly recognise them.

'Gramps, Grandma Minnie!' I call out with great excitement as I run across to them. 'I knew I would see you very soon.'

We put our arms around one another and are overcome with emotion. Tears of joy run down our faces. We're so happy.

'Jamie, it's wonderful to be with you again. We just heard from one of the angels that you had arrived,' Grandma says, as she gives me a big kiss on my cheek and another hug.

We sit down on the sofas and I look at my grandparents almost in disbelief. How easy it is for me to remember those familiar looks; the smiling blue eyes of Gramps with his short fair hair, and the tanned face of Grandma with her soft brown eyes. Because I have two grandmas she was known in the family as Grandma Minnie, and she's my dad's mother. My grandad's name is Richard, but I've always known him as Gramps. We begin to talk and laugh about some of the times we spent together in the past. It soon feels as if we've hardly been apart.

When I was just a child, Gramps and Grandma would often visit our family home in Abingdon, near Oxford, England. I always loved the stories about Jesus that Gramps would read to me, before I went to bed.

I remind my grandma of the day I told her some great news.

'Grandma, do you remember the time when I cycled over to your Victorian, terraced cottage in Newbury? I was just seventeen years old at the time. We sat together at the dining room table sharing tea and scones, and I told you that I'd become a Christian.

'Jamie, I will always remember that day,' she replies.

I tell her, 'I never forgot your reply, Grandma. You said, with great certainty, Jesus would never leave me, and one day I would be with him in heaven.'

Grandma looks at me, and with shining eyes says, 'Oh yes Jamie, and you will meet him. The Lord is here.'

Gramps tells me about some of the other family members in heaven, who they see regularly.

He says, 'You'll meet our other son, your Uncle Frank, who you remember died while climbing in Snowdonia, and there are your two great aunts, Alma and Annie.'

'What about my niece, Karen? Is she here too? She always had a smile for everyone, despite being so severely disabled and wheelchair-bound. She was an inspiration to all who knew her. I think she was just twelve when she died.'

Grandma smiles and says, 'Yes, Karen is here. We see her all the time. In fact she's now one of the youth dancers.'

'It will be great to see Karen and everyone else,' I respond, as I think about the times I last saw each of them.

Gramps gets up, walks over to one of the tall windows and looks out. He turns to me while waving with his hand saying, 'It's just over there, God's great Throne Room. You'll meet the Lord there. He's surrounded by a multitude of angels, and you'll see the seven archangels who stand in front of the throne. The light in the Throne Room is the brightest anywhere and the golden colours are magnificent. The presence of God is incredible and the power of his love is wonderful.'

I walk over with Grandma to join him, and he points out various large buildings in the distance. One of the buildings has an enormous honey-gold dome.

Gramps begins to describe the scene. 'In the centre of heaven surrounding God's Throne Room is a cluster of beautiful buildings, which stand out from all the others. Each structure is made from a different gemstone with a unique shape and colour. Viewed by the angels from high above, these special buildings appear like the jewels of a royal crown, which has been placed upon the city. This is the diadem of the New Jerusalem.'

'That must look stunning,' I respond.

'I'm sure your dad taught you all about the different gemstones, didn't he? asks Gramps.

'Yes, he did,' I reply. 'But, what you probably don't know Gramps, is that after leaving school I went to university and qualified as an architect. I'm also passionate about building design. What I've already seen is unbelievable, so I can't wait to see all these other places for myself.'

Gramps smiles to himself and pauses while deep in thought.

He responds, 'Heaven was designed and built by the greatest architect of all, God himself. The more you know about the architect the greater your understanding of the designs.'

We spend ages looking out across the city. I feel so comforted to be reunited with these two wonderful people. I think about the different members of my own family, who also believed in Jesus as their Saviour. In heaven we are all brothers and sisters of one big church family. We are all citizens of the kingdom of heaven.

Eventually Gramps says, 'We'd better be going.'

Looking at me he says, 'We'll see you again very soon, Jamie.' We hug each other and they leave the apartment.

I walk back to the window to take another look out across the city; the colours sparkle like jewels. Deep in my heart there's one thing I know more than anything else. I want to visit the Throne Room, to worship God and see Jesus Messiah for myself. I don't think I'll be waiting for long.

THE THRONE ROOM

No sooner have Gramps and Grandma gone, than Thaniel my angel friend is back.

'Jamie, it's time to go again,' he calls out, inviting me with an urgent wave of his hand.

Leaving the apartment, we enter the courtyard where several children are singing and laughing together, as they hold hands and dance in a circle around the fountain.

I ask Thaniel, 'Where are we going?'

He says, 'I'm taking you to God's Throne Room. You'll be in the presence of Almighty God, enthroned in his glory, and meet Jesus, the Messiah. I promise, you'll have a wonderful time.'

I reply, 'To finally meet with God face to face. I'm ready and I can't wait.'

We set off through the courtyard and along the network of paths between the mansion blocks. Soon, we reach tree-lined Rachel Avenue, which runs along the south side of the canal. Plenty of people are out walking and busily chatting. A group of teenage girls are giggling together, as they stand on one of the canal's many small, arched bridges. Many citizens are sitting on the carved white-crystal benches, positioned on either side of the waterway. As we walk on I spot Gramps and Grandma, sitting with some friends, on the opposite side of the canal. I wave at them, and they immediately wave back with big smiles. I tell Thaniel about their visit to my apartment, and repeat all they told me about the special places in the city centre.

Thaniel says, 'The city is a place of infinite beauty and unparalleled design. You'll be amazed at what you see.'

While doing my architectural degree, I visited some stunning cities like Bath, Edinburgh, London, Paris and Barcelona. But these places pale into insignificance compared to heaven.

The magnificent buildings on both sides of the avenue are mostly luxury apartments; like the one that's my new home. They are set well back behind neat gardens, which run the length of the avenue. The gardens are filled with trees and beautiful, flowering shrubs set in rich, green lawns. As I breathe in the sweet-scented fragrance, I think of my dad who was always out in the garden, busy keeping the grass cut - especially for Mum.

I ask Thaniel, 'Who keeps the lawns looking so trim?'

He laughs and says, 'This is heaven. Here the grass lives but never grows; it's always the same length. Heaven was created for eternity, there's no ageing, no decay and nothing wears out. Everything is sustained by the eternal nature and power of God. It's the same for all the citizens - no one grows older, you remain the same age as when you first arrived. Everyone is free from pain, disease and disability, and you never get tired or stressed. That's why many older people appear younger than they really are. Later on, you'll discover much more about time in heaven.'

As we reach a busy road junction, Thaniel points to his left and says, 'We go this way to the city centre and Throne Square.'

We turn into Issachar Street and cross the bridge over the canal. I lean over the edge to look into the crystal-clear water. This is the same highway we took from Assembly Square, when I first arrived. The whole length of the street is paved with glistening gold, in more of those beautiful symmetric patterns. Hundreds of citizens are out and about, with several angels among them.

'How far is it to Throne Square?' I ask Thaniel.

'It's quite some distance, but we'll be there in no time - you'll see,' he replies confidently.

I feel totally excited about the prospect of entering the Throne Room, being in the holy presence of God, and seeing Jesus my Saviour for the first time. However, deep down I still feel a little apprehensive.

When I meet God, my heavenly Father in person, how will I react? Will we have a conversation? I wonder to myself.

Recognising the thoughtful expression on my face, Thaniel says, 'Meeting God face to face in the Throne Room is the most wonderful moment a Christian can experience. As angels, we also love to spend time there; when we're not on other missions. It will change you forever. Citizens, both young and old, love to meet with God again and again.'

I glance back at Thaniel with a half smile, and feel reassured by his words.

I remember the occasion, shortly before my eighteenth birthday, when I became a Christian at an Easter camp meeting. From that moment, I started to learn more about God and the new life within me. I began to understand about the new birth and being born again from above. My spiritual experience was only made possible when I personally accepted the truth about Jesus.

I believed that he was God's Son, the promised Messiah, and that he came to earth to establish the kingdom of heaven. I realised that on a personal level, I fell far short of God's standards. Jesus was put to death on the cross to take the punishment I deserved. But the Messiah rose from the dead and then went back to heaven as Lord. He promised to prepare a place in heaven for his followers, so we could be with him forever. Now I am here and about to see him for myself.

I look around at the beautiful buildings on either side of the street, which are made from sea-green crystal. The light reflecting on the walls creates brilliant displays of blue, teal and turquoise. Many properties are constructed like my own place, with large windows and balustraded verandas. Everything is spotless, there's no dust, no litter and no pollution. The pure air is filled with the sweet fragrance of blossom.

After crossing Miriam Avenue with its own picturesque canal, we walk through Fountain Square; a beautiful quadrangle with gardens and fountains. The central fountain is carved out of white crystal and stands some seven metres tall. This elegant fountain has a series of six crystal bowls, each one wider than the one above, to catch and cascade the sparkling water. Walking close by, I feel the fine spray on my face and the sound of the gentle splashing almost whispers with life.

I soon start to notice the impressive buildings towering around us. Names are inscribed over the entrances to some of them. The large, emerald-green building opposite us is identified as the LIBRARY. Great crowds now fill the city centre streets; there's a constant buzz of conversation and the sound of singing is never far away.

Thaniel points and says, 'Look! There's the dome of the Throne Room.'

Up close, the massive, golden dome of the Throne Room looks stunning. I've seen the dome before, but only from a distance. Now I can appreciate the true scale and height of this most important, holy place.

Thaniel continues, 'The time has come for your face to face encounter with Almighty God and with Messiah, who is King of kings and the Lord of lords. This is where the presence of God resides and from where he rules his kingdom. You'll see Jesus, the Son of God, standing at God's right hand. I'll take you to the entrance and will be just outside when you return.'

A shiver goes through me as I think about what I'm about to experience. This will be an encounter like no other, and one I expect I will never forget. Flashing through my mind are times in the past when I talked with God in prayer. When I asked my heavenly Father to meet the needs of those close to me, and to help me through difficult days. Memories return of the many occasions I offered praise to God when attending my church, I sang the hymns and worship songs and sometimes played the piano keyboard.

One of the most vivid times of worship was at a New Wine Festival, two years after becoming a Christian. The presence of God was so real at the camp that year. On the Friday evening, we all knelt down on the muddy floorboards and the Holy Spirit came down and filled us all with peace and joy. I was a much stronger Christian after that particular week.

The sight of Throne Square is awesome. The blue sapphire of the central plaza sparkles like a sea of glass, and reflects many of the shapes and colours of the surrounding buildings. In the middle of the vast plaza is the centrepiece of heaven - God's Throne Room. The colossal, circular domed structure dominates the square and most of the city centre. Built with precious Chrysolite, its translucent, honey-gold walls rise over seventy metres high to the crest of the dome. This is by far the tallest structure I've seen in heaven - it's unbelievable!

The diameter of the Throne Room is a massive three hundred metres. The scale of this building easily rivals any similar shaped structure on earth, whether ancient or modern.

'The Throne Room is enormous. How many people does it hold?' I ask Thaniel.

He replies, 'The Throne Room is large enough to accommodate up to 100,000 worshippers. Of course, citizens are arriving and leaving all the time.'

Across the plaza are clusters of small trees in blossom. Some are pink; others white and a few are blue. There's also a series of water fountains springing up in sequence from small holes in the crystal floor. Several of the city's great highways can be seen converging on the square; bringing citizens from all directions.

Looking up to the pale yellow sky, I see enormous crowds of shining angels, almost motionless as they wait their turn to enter. Their white robes are bathed in soft golden light, and their faces are fixed toward the Throne Room. High up in the wall and just below the dome is a circular balcony with narrow openings. I watch as the angels constantly enter and leave.

Thaniel explains, 'Citizens can enter the Throne Room by any of the four main entrances set at each compass point. We will enter from the south.'

Thaniel and I make our way up the three shallow steps, and begin to walk across the plaza's expansive concourse. I feel as if I'm being drawn towards the Throne Room.

Among the large crowds are young people, children, and even tiny babies being carried by angels. I recognise the faces of some of the people, who I saw shortly before I entered the city. I spot the couple carrying their young son, just as they did at the city entrance. In front of me is the fair-haired teenage girl, I'd also seen at the gate. Hundreds of people are also leaving the Throne Room. Their faces look radiant, and as if in a dream, they appear totally oblivious to everyone else around them. I feel a growing excitement. At last I feel ready to meet the Lord.

As we arrive at the south entrance of the Throne Room all conversation ceases and there's a remarkable silence. The wide-open doors are adorned with an exquisite design of precious gemstones in primary colours. Deep-blue sapphires border a cluster of ruby-red sardius, which surround a display of yellow citrine in the shape of a star.

I look for Thaniel, but he's disappeared. I go in alone. Unsure of what to expect I'm reluctant to even lift my eyes. As I follow the others, I look down at the blue crystal steps beneath my feet. I'm overwhelmed by the all-powerful presence of God, and the intense golden light shining all around me. It's the same radiance that shone at the Issachar Gate, but now it's so much more intense.

I feel God's light shining into every recess of my being; he sees everything and all is revealed. My thoughts, my intentions, my motives and my memories are all subject to his searching gaze. He knows me better than I know myself, just as he has done since before I was born.

But in these moments, I experience no fear of his power or condemnation under his justice. This is because I know, without a doubt, my heavenly Father has always loved me and wanted me to be his child.

Glancing either side of me, I see huge numbers of people packed into the tiered stands. When I reach the floor of the main arena, I keep walking forward and somehow manage to pick my way slowly through the vast crowd. Although there are tens of thousands of people in the Throne Room, I'm urged on by a deep desire to be in God's very presence.

It's my journey, and I want to be ready for my personal encounter with God. My mind is very focussed on the fact that this is likely to be the most important meeting I will ever have with the Lord. At last, I find a place well inside the enormous room and with my head still lowered I stand still.

My heart feels as if it's melting in God's presence; I have no desire to resist. All my inner strength and motivation is evaporating. I fall to my knees in total surrender. The reality of God's presence is way beyond anything I've ever experienced or even imagined. My bowed head rests between my outstretched hands, on the cool, crystal floor beneath me. I have nothing. I am empty.

Compared to the greatness of God, I consider myself as a mere grain of sand. I can't speak. I can't cry. I can't even move. I stay just where I am and worship. There's nothing else to do.

How long I remained on my knees before God is impossible to know. Time isn't important anyway. A new reality dawns upon my mind. It's not about how I see myself, but rather how God feels about me. The truth is that he sees me as his precious child; he values me and counts me as a jewel in his crown. An incredible feeling of calm is now covering me and soaking into every part of my being. I'm resting in God's presence and totally at peace. A faint smile crosses my face as I think about the epitaph often inscribed on gravestones - Rest in Peace.

From my crouched position, I slowly stretch back my legs and lie prostrate, still face down, with my arms resting at my side. I'm vaguely aware of others, kneeling or lying down around me. I stay just where I am for a long time.

A fresh wave of joy flows over me, directly from the presence of God. It fills me from the top of my head to the tip of my toes. I can only describe this as awesome joy in God's presence. As I remain lying down, I experience being washed repeatedly with soothing surges of love, joy and peace. This is so wonderful, and I just want to stay here.

Eventually, I lift myself up and while kneeling, I raise up my hands. Feeling my strength renewed, I lift my head up for the first time and open my eyes. I get my first glimpse of God's majesty and begin to gaze at the face of the Almighty, seated high upon his throne.

Pure joy is now flowing through me with incredible energy. I smile constantly at God, as his love pours like a waterfall into the depths of my empty heart. Every part of me feels his transforming power.

I realise what I'm experiencing, and my heart cries out, 'This is God's glory.'

My heavenly Father is sharing his own glory with me, his child. I'm being absorbed by the very presence of God and incapable of further response.

I recall reading in the Scriptures about the life we receive from God. While on earth it's just a foretaste, like a starter. It's meant to give us an appetite for the fullness awaiting us in heaven. I'm now starting to experience this abundance for myself. Wow!

I can't take my eyes away from the crystal-white brilliance of God's dazzling appearance, which is encircled by flaming orange and radiates with crimson red. At the sides of the throne, scores of cherubim cluster tightly together like royal guards within the glory cloud. Their wings are wrapped around so closely that they appear to hold up the very throne itself.

Directly over God's throne, a bright emerald rainbow shines powerfully through the rising clouds of pale haze. It's far more vivid and luminous than anything I've seen before. Around me, I hear deep echoes of thunder and see frequent flashes of golden lightning. High above God's throne, a large group of angelic seraphim hover in a unified formation; their outspread wings form a bright shimmering canopy.

All around the huge dome of the Throne Room, many thousands of angels are bathed in golden light. Positioned in regiments, ranks and rows, they worship God and wait to serve him.

I wonder, 'Did Thaniel join the hosts of angels that were waiting outside the Throne Room?'

In front of me, seven tall angels are stood facing the throne. These must be the archangels Gramps mentioned. I watch as they quickly come and go from the throne as servants of God.

'Where do they go?' I wonder.

As ministers of God's government they wait for divine instructions. The sight of these very powerful angelic beings fulfilling God's commands fills me with awe and causes me to shudder.

The sudden arrival of four, unusual angels startles me. They present themselves before the throne. Each one has a striking appearance, with a very distinctive face and three pairs of iridescent white wings. The first one has a face like a lion, the second looks like an ox, the third has a man's face and the fourth one resembles an eagle.

'Are these the four living ones that Thaniel mentioned?' I ask myself.

In contrast to the archangels, who stand still to face the throne, these heavenly beings constantly move around, turning towards the Lord and also observing our worship. I'm gripped with intrigue about their purpose.

The drama of the Throne Room continues to unfold. From the far right, a long line of distinguished-looking men slowly approaches the throne. Each one of them is wearing a golden crown and a white robe, adorned with a purple sash. They sit down on a row of small white thrones set out in a semi-circle behind the archangels. It occurs to me these men are the first apostles of the church such as Peter, James and John sitting together with the twelve sons of Israel.

Around God's throne, the cloud of glory thickens and becomes brighter as another figure comes into sight from within. Fixing my gaze, I see for myself the appearance of the Lamb of God, Messiah Jesus. He stands as a man on the right hand side of God, his Father. The glory upon him is so intense that his head and hair are shining as white as snow. His face glows with the brilliance of the sun, and his eyes burn with fire. He is dressed in the purest of white robes, which radiate with penetrating light. Across his chest is a bright golden sash; his hands and feet glow like polished bronze. In his right hand he's holding a shining bronze sword, and in the other he grasps a ringed set of large, golden keys.

This is the same Jesus, who lived his life on earth, died on the cross and was raised back to life. Now I see him for myself in heaven, the Son of God, Messiah, appointed as Lord of lords and King of kings. He is the

Head of the true church and the Firstborn in heaven. He stands triumphant, victorious. I'm thrilled to see him!

Every eye is focussed on Jesus and citizens again fall to their knees. I join the thousands around me in a period of incredible worship, as we gaze at our Saviour. The archangels in front of the throne bow down in adoration. The elders on the thrones also fall to their knees before God and lay their crowns on the crystal floor. An awesome silence fills the room, and only the steady fluttering sound of seraphic wings can be heard high above us. Smoke billows up around the throne and almost envelops the watchful cherubim.

The truth about worship explodes as new revelation in my mind. My fragile, earthly understanding is shattered once and for all. It's what we do when we meet the Lord in spirit and in truth. In the power and absolute holiness of his presence - there's nothing we can do but worship. No songs, no words, no movement is necessary - just worship.

A small golden altar, about one metre high, stands directly in front of God's throne. Incense is burning in its shallow tray. A narrow trail of white smoke rises before the throne, adding to the pale haze above.

High overhead one of the seraphim calls out in a loud voice.

'The Spirit and the Bride say "Come!" and let him who hears say, "Come".'

The sound of the beating wings of the seraphim intensifies, and then they all respond loudly together.

'Let the one who is thirsty come, and whoever desires, let them take the water of life.'

Immediately, I understand that the prayers of the church, the Bride of Messiah on earth, are joining the prayers of the Spirit at God's throne. I feel the same prayer rising in my own heart, and almost before I realise it, I'm also calling out.

'Amen, let it be, amen, let it be.'

Right across the great assembly, citizens stand to affirm the prayer of the church.

Suddenly, Messiah steps forward and declares loudly and with great authority.

'I am the beginning and the end of everything. I am the Living One, though once I was dead, now I am alive for ever'.

The recognition of his power is absolute. As he speaks, the crystal floor vibrates and the cherubim tremble. Everyone, including the archangels and the honourable men, falls again to their knees, and bows down with their faces to the ground.

After a long silence, one of the honourable elders begins to call out repeatedly, 'Worthy, worthy, worthy are you our Lord and our God to receive glory, honour and power.'

More of the honourable men join in, and then they all stand together with their arms raised. They declare in unison, 'Worthy are you, our Lord and our God, to receive glory, honour and power. For you have created everything, and because of your word all things exist.'

Far above me, I hear again the rushing sound of wings fluttering, as the seraphim respond with praises and proclamations.

They cry out, 'Holy, holy, holy is the Lord God the Almighty, who was, and who is, and who is to come.'

I stand to join in with many of the other worshippers and repeat the phrase, 'Holy, holy, holy is the Lord God the Almighty, who was, and who is, and who is to come.'

More clouds of white vapour rise around the throne, almost hiding the faithful cherubim. Then a great chorus of song fills the room, as the heavenly choir overhead sings out.

'Hallelujah, for the Lord our God the Almighty reigns.'

The sound is almost deafening. Everyone is now standing. I notice crowns spread across the floor. To my right, I see children aged as young as three, with eyes wide open. Their little faces look up, as they lift their hands in praise. I willingly raise my arms high, as an act of adoration to Almighty God.

My gaze returns to Jesus, just as two of the cherubim move from the base of the throne, and stand facing him. From under their wings they reach out their open hands. Jesus gives to one of them his ring of keys, and then offers his sword to the other. They stand either side of the Messiah and raise the keys and sword high over their heads, facing us with outstretched wings.

Jesus steps forward; he opens out his arms to reveal the palms of his hands. Dark purple scars in the palms of his hands are clearly visible. Jesus views the great congregation from the floor to the ceiling and from left to right. Then, he looks directly at me, and his loving eyes burn into my spirit.

I breathe out, 'My Lord, my God,' as I capture forever the vision of his face. Every previous image of Jesus stored in my mind evaporates, as hope gives way to reality.

He calls out across the great room and his voice echoes around the dome.

'Do not be afraid. I am the First and the Last. I am the Living One; I was dead, and now look, I am alive forever and ever! And I hold the keys of Death and Hades. I am the root and offspring of David, the Bright and Morning Star.'

The angels immediately respond and cry out, 'Hallelujah, salvation and glory, and honour and power belong to the Lord our God.'

The congregation repeats the proclamation, 'Hallelujah, salvation and glory, and honour and power belong to the Lord our God.'

This happens several times getting louder and louder. Finally the myriad of watching angels break out in song with the Hallelujah Chorus. The whole place erupts with loud cheering, shouts, whoops, jumps, whistles and much clapping of hands.

I think to myself, how much I would have valued an encounter like this with the living God while on earth. I wonder how different my life might have been. But then I'm reminded that on earth we lived by faith, we believed in things that couldn't be seen. At best we got a glimpse of future glory. I silently pray that my family, friends and everyone else who knows me, will keep faith with what God has said in the Scriptures.

Eventually Jesus lowers his raised hands and the music becomes much quieter. The cherubim return the sword and keys to Messiah and return to their places around the throne. High up in the dome, the angels bring their gentle adoration to God and his son, Messiah Jesus. They sing the same phrase over and over again, using a simple melody.

'Worthy, worthy, worthy is the Lamb who was slain.'

Many around me softly join in the song. It's then I notice something unusual. Water is flowing from under the throne. Just in front of the archangels is a small stream of water. It runs silently across the blue floor in a shallow gulley, past the archangels and the honourable men, towards the eastern entrance of the Throne Room. It appears to be coming from God's throne, in front of the Lord Jesus. As I watch, one of the cherubim hands Jesus a small, crystal bowl. Taking the bowl, he bends down and dips it into the shallow pool of water. Messiah begins to offer a refreshing sip to a line of waiting worshippers.

I step forward to join the growing queue - a rarity in heaven! Children, youths and adults wait in turn to taste the heavenly water. I walk past the row of thrones, and pass between the archangels. As my place in the line advances, I think about the earlier call of the seraphim and the invitation by the Messiah himself.

'Let the one who is thirsty come, and whoever desires, let them take the water of life.'

I don't have long to wait. Jesus carefully lowers the bowl again into the water, and raises it to my lips. His warm brown eyes pour love into my heart.

Quietly, he says to me, 'Jamie, drink the water of life.'

It's as if it was just Jesus and myself, alone.

'Thank you Lord,' I reply.

I place my lips over the edge of the thin crystal bowl, and take a sip of the cool water. Immediately I feel a surge of divine power through my body.

I turn and retrace my steps among the audience. Kneeling down again, I close my eyes and quietly give thanks to God for all he's done, and his gift of eternal life.

I realise my time in the Throne Room is ending. So I start to slowly make my way across the arena, back through the crowds of worshippers. I climb the steps and exit on the south side. Once outside, I cross the bustling plaza, and just hope I'm going in the right direction. Waiting for me at the plaza steps, with a hint of a smile, is my faithful friend, Thaniel. I'm so pleased to see him.

'Thaniel, that was awesome,' I exclaim as he waits to see my reaction. 'To be in the presence of God like that is unforgettable. My heart just melted when I saw Jesus Messiah, especially when he showed us his scarred hands. I drank the water of life. Oh, and to hear the angels worshipping God was amazing.'

'I was there too,' says Thaniel. 'I managed to slip in and join them for a while. It was just before we sang the Hallelujah Chorus,' he adds with a look of satisfaction.

'Would you like to go to the Library next time? asks Thaniel.

'That would be great,' I reply.

'I'll call at your apartment. I must go now, as I've some other matters to attend to,' he explains.

He disappears into the crowd, and I'm left to make my way back to my own place along Issachar Street. This has been an occasion I will never forget.

THE LIBRARY

It's no surprise to discover that the city of God has a library, to house all the records, books and scrolls mentioned in the Bible. I'm very much looking forward to my first visit. I expect the Library will become a regular haunt, as I become more familiar with my new surroundings. My thinking is partly based on previous visits to libraries while on earth. As a child, I always looked forward to my weekly trips to exchange story books at the local library. I loved to spend time browsing the titles on the shelves, and selecting books that appealed to my interests and imagination. Occasionally, I had the added delight of listening to stories being read aloud by animated storytellers, while we all sat down on the carpet.

During my three years as a university student, I was always going to the academic libraries. Often, I lost all track of time becoming absorbed with reading and research for my architectural studies. The reality of so much useful information gathered in one place was for me an inspiration.

Thaniel arrives at the doorway to my apartment, just as he had promised.

'Ready for your visit to the Library?' he calls out.

'Oh yes, I am,' I reply without any hesitation.

We set off together along the path and walk along the avenue, in the direction of the city centre. Everywhere we go there's great joy, with frequent sounds of laughter and many happy-looking people engaged in conversation. I'm now feeling much more relaxed about heaven, and everything is such a pleasure.

'Listen, what's that?' I suddenly ask Thaniel, hoping he will know.

Up ahead, there's the unmistakable sound of horses' hooves approaching, and people cheering. We quickly arrive at the main

39

junction where Rachel Avenue crosses Issachar Street. All around the edge of the square, crowds of people both young and old are shouting and waving. I can see what appears to be a parade taking place, and it's heading towards the city centre along Issachar Street. Hundreds of horse-drawn chariots are being driven by angels, who are stood on the rear steps. The cheering crowds, the trotting horses, and the clatter of chariot wheels running along the gold paving, creates an exciting noise. The faces of the angel charioteers are fixed firmly ahead as they speed by, without a single wave or even a glance toward the crowds on either side. Outstretched arms tightly grip the reins, which steer their stylish, white stallions. Hurrying by in rows of three, the golden chariots gleam like flames of fire driven by the wind.

Thaniel raises his voice above the din to explain. 'These warrior angels are returning from the success of another completed mission on earth, and must report directly to Angel Headquarters from where they were sent. There's a viewing gallery for citizens at the headquarters. I'll take you there some time if you want; I'm sure you'll love it.'

'That does sound good,' I respond, trying to visualise the scene at HQ.

The last lines of chariots speed by and the crowds quickly disperse in all directions, leaving the square in relative peace. Thaniel and I continue our journey, first crossing over the canal and then making our way along highway towards the Library. I think to myself about all those warrior angels, riding their chariots through the lower heavens close to the earth. I realise angels must be given many different tasks on the earth, although their work is rarely seen by human eyes. I feel privileged to have seen them for myself.

The long walk to the Library gives us both time to chat. Thaniel asks me about the books I've read - apart from the Bible of course! I spend time explaining to him about one of my favourite books - The Lion, the Witch and the Wardrobe by C.S. Lewis. To my surprise, Thaniel tells me that he's already heard about the story, and knows all about Aslan and the land of Narnia.

We reach our destination in the city centre and Thaniel stops at the corner of Library Square, with its trees and fountains. We both stand to admire the impressive appearance of the Library and its grounds, which are enclosed by a high wall. This five-storey rectangular building is made from emerald, and its translucent, green walls shine with a welcoming light. The mansard-style, white crystal roof has two slopes on each of its four sides, the lower slope being steeper than the upper slope. A row of dormer windows with golden balconies adds elegance to the lower slopes of the roof.

As we cross the square, crowds of people are coming and going from the main entrance to the building. We follow a small group of visitors, and climb the six shallow steps, which extend across the length of the Library's front facade. The large inscription LIBRARY, in the headstone over the entrance, confirms we're at the right place.

We pass through the arched entrance, which is flanked by two small rectangular doors. Walking from the lobby along the wide corridor, I peer through the clear bluish-green crystal walls. On either side there are large rooms, which are crowded with people. I look back for Thaniel, only to realise he's disappeared again. I'm getting used to his unannounced comings and goings.

As I enter the great hall of the Library, the sheer scale of the place is most impressive. The large, rectangular space I'm standing in measures at least sixty metres long and around forty metres wide. It appears to be surrounded by various rooms, which are laid out on five different levels. The Library's shining, crystal floor is paved with perfectly joined slabs of sea-green beryl. Light floods the whole room through the misty-white crystal roof, which is spread out high above us. Looking up, I can see that on each level there are gallery walkways with carved balustrades. Scores of people are briskly walking along the galleries, which extend all the way around the walls of the hall. A handful of visitors have paused to look around the vast space, and can be seen observing those of us on the ground below.

I walk across to one of the alcoves; the compartments are packed full of ancient papyrus scrolls. The pristine white scrolls vary in size and most have central rods with golden ends; the titles are written on little hanging tags. I gaze along the walls at the countless shelves, which reach from floor to ceiling on every level. There are hundreds of thousands, probably millions of books and scrolls deposited here.

There's a constant hum of conversation among the many hundreds of people, who are busily criss-crossing the hall in all directions. A few citizens are sitting around on seats set beside large bookcases, and some are occupied reading documents. I spot angels moving among the crowds, with their characteristic white shining hair and robes. Some of them are carrying books, while others hold tied bundles of scrolls under their arms. It makes me think some angels must work as heavenly couriers.

'Hello there, is this your first visit?' says a man nearby.

Turning around, I see a middle-aged man stood next to me.

'Err, yes ...isn't this place magnificent?' I reply.

I guess he's thinking I look a bit lost; hardly anybody is just standing around like me.

'My name's Lucas. Would you like me to tell you about the Library and show you around?' he asks.

Lucas appears friendly, and I instantly get the impression he's well-informed about the Library.

'That would be great,' I respond, adding, 'Oh, and I'm Jamie.'

Lucas smiles and his eyes shine bright as he begins to point out the main features of the Library. He shows me the different gallery levels, and is keen to mention the raised platform at the far end of the great hall.

He points to the platform and explains, 'From time to time an archangel is sent from the Throne Room. He's given an order by God, to collect one of the sacred books or sealed scrolls stored here in the Library. A small number of scrolls have been sealed with an imprint of clay, after being rolled up and tied. The dried clay seal must be broken before the scroll can be untied and its contents read.'

He continues, 'Whenever an archangel arrives at the Library, he stands and waits at the entrance just behind the platform. When this happens, an angelic trumpet fanfare is played from the Library's top gallery. Complete silence then fills the whole building. Everyone in the hall and along the galleries turns to face the platform and stands perfectly still. The archangel then steps up to the platform and calls out for the title of the requested sealed scroll - everyone waits.'

'Within a short space of time, an angel appears at one of the six doors into the great hall. Following the lead angel is a second angel, who carries the requested document held up over his head. A third angel also enters just behind. They make their way to the platform and the scroll is held up in front of the archangel. The scroll title shown on the hanging tag is carefully checked. Then the archangel turns to leave the hall and returns to the Throne Room, along with the three attendant angels who carry the scroll.'

Lucas explains to me, 'Only someone with authority is counted worthy to break open the seals. The honourable elders, who stand before God, have to agree who that person should be. One of the special scrolls kept here in the Library is known as the Scroll of Judgement. This is the only scroll sealed with seven clay seals. We are waiting for this scroll to be called for at anytime. When each of those seals are broken, catastrophic events, which have been foretold, will take place on the earth.'

I'm fascinated by everything Lucas is telling me about the Library. I can't wait to look around.

He tells me, 'I was born in Syria, and was privileged to go to school in the city of Antioch. From a very early age I loved to read and write, and went on to train as a doctor. After becoming a Christian, I became close friends of Paul and Barnabus, who were leaders in the Antioch church. I often wrote to them and kept in touch during their missionary journeys.

Suddenly, it dawns on me who Lucas is, and I feel hugely honoured to be with him.

Lucas continues, 'One day I had a vision from God, in which I saw myself writing a book about the life of Jesus. The problem was that I hadn't actually met Jesus in person. So I spent many months travelling around and doing interviews with those who had known him. I met many reliable eye-witnesses in Jerusalem, Judea and Galilee. Based on my notes about their stories, I wrote my own account of the life and work the Messiah. I found the experience so enjoyable, that I went on to write about the early days of the church and the apostles - especially my friends, Paul and Barnabas.'

'Lucas, I really appreciate you telling me about yourself. You are the first citizen I've met who's mentioned in the Bible.'

I give him a friendly hug. Secretly, I'm really excited to be in the presence of such an influential person. Just wait until Gramps and Grandma get to hear, and I suppose Thaniel will be quite interested too.

'I offered to show you around Jamie, follow me this way,' Lucas says with a quick wave of his hand.

We weave our way across the bustling concourse towards one of arched doorways. My famous guide explains that there are six doorways on the ground floor, and each one leads through to a different reading room. As we pass through a short corridor, I notice lots of people using an ornate staircase leading to the floors above. The balustraded stairs are carved from red and white striped onyx. We remain on the ground floor, and after passing the stairwell we reach the first of the reading rooms.

Facing us is a long reception desk with several angels in conversation with citizens. An assortment of scrolls, books and manuscripts are spread out along the polished quartz countertop. The rest of the large room is filled with people, who are busily moving around and carrying all kinds of documents. Visitors are standing at many of the two-metre square desks, which are positioned symmetrically across the room. In one corner, I spot a small group of children all looking very closely at an opened scroll with some colourful drawings.

The room is mostly quiet with a few hushed whispers, the rustle of papyrus and an occasional gasp of surprise. Everyone is totally occupied with their reading; some are gently loosening the ties and unrolling scrolls while others are carefully leafing through their books.

I ask Lucas, 'Is anyone allowed to read books in here?

'Yes, of course,' he replies. 'You can ask to read all sorts of records. There are even books that have been specially written for children. Many records are very old, and some are even inscribed on stone or clay tablets. However, no one is allowed to read the sealed books or special scrolls, like those reserved for the Throne Room.'

Lucas explains, 'Within the Library there are hundreds of thousands of papyrus scrolls, parchments and books that can be read. These are the official records, including the Books of Remembrance about people and events on the earth. More records are being added all the time. Records are also kept of the activity of angels, but these are stored at their own headquarters.'

'So how can I take a look?' I ask.

'You simply wait your turn at the desk and then ask one of the angels. He goes off and in no time returns with your request. Although sometimes, the document you want may already be displayed on one of the tables.'

Lucas continues, 'This particular reading room is known as the Honours Room. You may have noticed the small inscription over the entrance as we came in.'

'No, I missed that; I probably got distracted by the amazing staircase. But what is meant by the Honours Room?' I ask.

'This room holds the records of achievement by God's people across the centuries. There are accounts of bravery, courage and selfless service by young and old alike. These records show how people have kept faith with what God has said, in spite of opposition and danger. They also tell of how Christians have advanced the kingdom of God on earth, even though it cost many of them their lives.' Lucas explains with passion.

I had no idea such detailed records were kept in heaven. This is mind-blowing.

'Why are all these records kept?' I ask Lucas.

He explains, 'Angels are tasked to watch over God's people, and also to take note of all important decisions made and actions undertaken. This applies to all who serve God, regardless of age or responsibility. This is very important work for the many thousands of angel scribes. These notes are then written up as official records. Much of this information is presented as evidence in the Hall of Honours. That is where each citizen stands before God, to give an account of their lives. During every crowning ceremony, extracts are read out publicly as citizens are honoured. You'll get an invitation to go there soon. I'll show you the Writing Room shortly, so you can watch the angel scribes as they work.'

'This is fascinating, so what about the other reading rooms of the Library?' I ask.

'Well,' replies Lucas, 'There's the Promise Room with a record of every promise God has ever made, whether to an individual, a nation, a church or a family. Then there's the Vocation Room, with details of every special gift and calling God has placed on someone's life. This includes teachers, doctors, scientists, artists, musicians, entrepreneurs, and leaders of church and state. You can also visit the Divine Plan room, to see records about God's purposes for the nations and his special plan for Israel. Another room is called the Church Room, where the records of all local churches and their leaders are stored. There are accounts of the faithfulness of church leaders, evangelists and missionaries, with complete details of their service for God.'

'The last reading room is the Revelation Room. This room contains records of every God-given prophecy and vision, with the name of the recipient along with the place and date. These records cover thousands of years, from the beginning of time, through the Bible ages, the medieval era and more recent centuries. There are often extra notes that show the resulting impact and influence of such prophecies. Many citizens are amazed when they read about the stories told in these particular records.'

'Lucas, this is incredible. I had no idea that all this important information was stored. I will definitely be returning to the reading rooms on a regular basis.'

'That's good, I'll be looking out for you,' replies Lucas.

I feel overcome with the absolute greatness of God. The Eternal One who is all-seeing, all-knowing and ever-present. The Lord, who holds each of us accountable for his gifts.

'Can we go upstairs?' I ask.

We make our way back out of the reading room, and I follow my distinguished guide up the ornate stairs. On the first level, we turn into a narrow gallery and check out the view of the great hall below. Behind us, there's row after row of large books lining the shelves. Each volume is beautifully bound and titled. I recognise on the book spines, the names of many cities and places around the world; they appear in alphabetical order. There are golden ladders nearby, to enable the books on the uppermost shelves to be reached.

We exit the gallery, walk past the stairwell and go through to another room. This time I notice the sign over the door, WRITING ROOM. Although it's similar in size to the reading room below, the layout is very different. A narrow walkway skirts right around the edge of the room. Most of the floor space is filled with small writing desks, each with a single stool. The desk tops are angled to around thirty degrees and measure about a square metre. Every desk displays its own writing kit. This includes an ink bottle with a hinged lid and a set of three golden reed pens in different lengths. There are also sheets of parchment and paper stored in an open drawer under each desk.

I can't help thinking back to my architect's studio in Abingdon. Little did I know it looked like a little bit of heaven!

Most of the desks are occupied by angels, who are busy writing their records with care and devotion. They appear oblivious to all other activity around them. The work takes place in complete silence, as onlookers move quietly along the outer aisles.

I watch one angel, who uses a fine needle to prick tiny holes into a sheet of parchment, to create a straight horizontal line for the writing. Another angel appears to copy notes from an assignment written in a cursive style and transcribe the detail on to a papyrus scroll using formal block capitals. We walk further round the room and Lucas nudges me gently.

He whispers, 'See how the angel is carefully selecting the horizontal woven line of the papyrus. This is to make sure the letters are perfectly sized and absolutely straight.'

I feel nervous just watching. I'm very glad it isn't me under such constant, public scrutiny.

At the far end of the room, we can see several angels handling scrolls. A five metre roll of joined papyrus sheets is being attached to a golden rod, and then slowly wrapped around it. The rod provides stability and a safe means of handling the scroll. Once the scroll is rolled up it can be tied and stored. Another angel is reading from a scroll. He unrolls it with one hand, and winds up the portion that has been read with his other hand. These papyrus rolls are being written in narrow columns, about ten centimetres wide and around forty lines of text, with single centimetre margins.

Along the walls next to the aisle are hundreds of scroll drawers. Each drawer contains about twelve scrolls, which have all been laid out horizontally. I notice the small label tags, identifying the contents, hanging from the end of each rod.

Lucas says, 'I'd like to show you another special place in the Library. Follow me.'

Leaving the Writing Room, we go up another flight of stairs to the second level. Lucas again leads the way along another gallery, until we pass through a doorway into a smaller room called the Treasury Room. There appears to be more angels than citizens in this particular room.

Lucas quietly explains, 'The Treasury Room is where the Holy Scriptures are kept. Each of the 39 scrolls of the Old Testament and 27 scrolls of the New Testament are on display.'

Taking me to a corner of the room where the gospels are stored, Lucas gently lifts out the copy of the Gospel he wrote. Opening the large scroll he begins to read the introductory paragraph.

'Inasmuch as many have undertaken to compile a narrative of the things that have been accomplished among us, just as those who from the beginning were eyewitnesses and ministers of the word have delivered them to us, it seemed good to me also, having followed all things closely for some time past, to write an orderly account for you, most excellent Theophilus, that you may have certainty concerning the things you have been taught.'

Lucas looks across at me, and his eyes fill with tears as he remembers writing his gospel.

'God chose "a nobody" like me to write these things. Little did I know that my account sent to Theophilus would become part of Holy Scripture. Praise the Lord of heaven and earth, who sent his son Jesus to bring salvation to all who believe.'

With great care, Lucas rolls the scroll back up and returns the Gospel to its place on the shelf. He then affectionately touches the tag at end of his other scroll, the Acts of the Apostles, which lies nearby.

He says, 'No promise of God is ever broken. God's will is done on earth, just as it is in heaven.'

As we make our away back along the corridor, I think about the importance of the Bible in my own life. Ever since becoming a believer, I longed to know more about God and his purposes for my life. I always accepted the truth of what the Bible said from Genesis to Revelation. My church taught that the Bible was the inspired word of God, and I believed it. My hope of eternal life was based on the reliability of the truth.

'There's one more scroll I want you to see,' says Lucas.

He brings me to a small, head-high opening in the wall along the corridor.

'Look in the window and tell me what you see?' suggests Lucas.

I peer in through the narrow opening, which is just about as wide as my head. In the room I can see an angel scribe writing line by line on a large new scroll. Two more angels stand nearby. I listen as one of the angels reads out each name and a place of birth, clearly spelling out each letter. The other angel watches, to observe that the words added are correct.

Lucas whispers, 'This is the Lamb's Book of Life, the place where the name of every believer in Jesus Messiah is recorded. Sometimes names are removed but that is very rare. There are hundreds of thousands of scrolls, which hold the names of citizens from across the nations. These records will be used in the Great Judgement.'

'Is my name written down somewhere in this room?' I ask.

He replies, 'Ask one of the angels for yourself.'

'Really?' I check with him.

'Yes, go on,' says Lucas.

I wait until the name being read out is fully written down and then I call out through the opening.

'Excuse me, ...excuse me, angels.'

All three angels turn and look at me, as I peer through the opening. They have a relaxed smile across their faces - as if this happens frequently. The angel scribe who was writing asks, 'How can we help you?'

'Well,' I say hesitantly, 'Can I see my own name written down in the Lamb's Book of Life?'

'What is your name, place and date of birth?' One of the other angels asks with efficiency.

I answer, 'My name is Jamie Ocklestone and was born on the 12th of April in 1981 in Abingdon, Oxfordshire, UK'

Almost before I've finished, the other angel disappears from view. In no time he returns with a long scroll, which he lays out facing toward me on a table, directly below the opening. I can read the title showing Oxfordshire 1980 - 1989. There's an awkward pause, as the angel slowly unrolls the scroll, lightly runs his finger down one of the columns, and suddenly stops.

'There you are young man,' says the angel with a hint of a smile.

I look down at the immaculate lettering JAMIE OCKLESTON - ABINGDON - APRIL 1981.

I was unprepared for my reaction on seeing my own name written in the Book of Life. Warm tears of gratitude run down my face, as I think about God's faithfulness, accepting me as his child. I'm overjoyed to see my very own name written down.

'Thank you so much,' I tell the angels, as they re-roll the scroll and return to their duties.

I stay and watch, as the angels continue their careful work, but get so preoccupied that I don't realise Lucas has been calling me.

He repeats himself with added emphasis, 'Jamie, come and see the children's gallery.'

I pull myself away from the viewing window, and follow Lucas up the stairs for two more levels to the fourth floor. As we arrive, there's a sudden burst of prolonged laughter coming from children further along the gallery. Lucas ushers me under an archway and into a lovely, bright room filled with happy little faces.

Over seventy children are listening with real interest to a story about Jesus; their eyes are glued on the popular storyteller. Sitting together are children from China, India, Africa, Europe and North America; their faces are lit up with smiles. Older kids squat down behind the younger ones and some as young as two sit cross-legged on the shiny, green floor. Positioned at the very front, I recognise the little boy who was carried by his parents into heaven. I'm so pleased to see him.

We slowly tip-toe our way to the back of the room, trying to avoid any distraction. Passing the shelves of books, I stand next to Lucas in a recessed alcove, well behind the children.

Lucas then whispers to me, with a nod toward the storyteller, 'That's Nick, he loves the children so much. He's always in here story-telling. You probably know him as Nicodemus, the Pharisee who was born again.'

'Wow,' I respond in a whisper. 'He's the man who met Jesus late one night, and had lots of questions about God's kingdom.'

'That's him,' Lucas says, 'He's a great friend of mine. I never knew him while I lived on earth. We actually met here in the Library. Nick has such an incredible memory, and he tells the children all about the miracles he saw Jesus perform.'

For a while we both listen, as Nick tells the children about the man born blind, and how Jesus restored his sight. I really like the moment he asks the children to shut their eyes tight, and think about a heaven without light. He then talks about his own spiritual blindness and how Jesus helped him to see the kingdom of God for himself.

As I hear Nick tell his story, I think about the difference Jesus has made to my life, and how I came to see the truth for myself.

Lucas nudges my arm, and in a low voice simply says, 'Follow me.'

Silently, we leave the children's gallery and climb a narrow set of steps to the top floor of the Library. The long narrow room isn't much wider than a corridor, and has a sloping ceiling. It's far less busy than the lower floors, with just a handful of other visitors. Here are the viewing balconies I'd noticed from the outside, when I first arrived.

Lucas brings me to the nearest dormer window; we step outside on the narrow ledge to enjoy the magnificent views across Library Square and the city. He points out Praise Pavilion and the Observatory not much further away. I pick out the some of the main highways leading away from the city centre, including Issachar Street. Row after row of beautiful buildings in stunning colours stretch out before us. Overhead, I see more angels travelling around; some flying on their own and others in small groups. I spend a long time with Lucas just watching the city life.

Eventually, Lucas says to me, 'Let's go back down stairs and take a walk in the Library garden?'

But first he's another feature to show me. At the far end of the narrow room is a tiny viewing stand, which looks down on the concourse of the great hall far below.

Lucas explains the detail, 'This is where the angel trumpeters play their fanfare, whenever the archangel arrives from the Throne Room.'

Pointing to a small external window, just visible between two angels, he says, 'One angel keeps a constant lookout for the arrival of the archangel, while the other one waits to sound the trumpet.'

Yet another task given to the angels, I think to myself.

'Lucas, that's really fascinating. Thanks for showing me.'

We go down several flights of stairs and finally emerge back in the great hall. Curiosity forces me to look up and identify the tiny stand. I can just see it high up and directly over the raised platform below. Lucas gives me a smile.

We then leave the main building through a narrow entrance, and I follow Lucas into a beautiful walled garden, which runs along the side of the Library. We walk along one of the narrow paths set between long rows of vines. Lucas pauses to pick a couple of juicy red grapes from a large hanging cluster. He passes one to me, as I wait behind him.

'Try this grape,' he says, 'They taste delicious.'

I accept the soft, ripe grape, and smelling its aroma I quickly pop it whole into my mouth. The sweetness of the rich flavour rests on my tongue and is deeply satisfying. It lingers for a few moments and then disappears.

'That was so delicious,' I tell Lucas, as we walk towards the end of the row.

'You'll taste more fruit of the vine at the Banqueting Hall,' he informs me.

I think to myself how wonderful that place must be - the Banqueting Hall.

I tell him, 'That sounds like a real party in heaven.' He nods with a big smile of agreement.

We reach a small golden door in the emerald wall. Lucas turns to me, hugs me and says, 'Jamie, it's been great to show you around. I know you'll be back soon, so do look out for me. I must leave you now to meet some other visitors. You can leave the garden by this door, whenever you are ready.'

I respond, 'It's been terrific to meet you Lucas, and to see so much of the Library. Thank you so much, I will be back.'

As I turn to leave, Lucas opens the door for me. Leaving the Library garden, I pass between some trees, and I'm soon back in Library Square. I think about everything I've seen and heard in the Library. My visit has given me a fresh understanding of heaven, and reminded me why making time count on earth was so important.

All those stored records about so many people, and even events yet to take place - it's quite incredible.

BENJAMIN STREET

I'm starting to find my own way around the city centre and already recognise many of the streets and larger buildings. According to Thaniel there are twelve main highways, which fan out from Throne Square in all directions, as far as the gates of the city. Gramps told me that one of these streets is supposed to be very different to all the rest, so I'm setting off to find out more. It's called Benjamin Street, and I've been told to begin my journey at the eastern side of the Throne Room.

After a long and pleasant stroll from my apartment along Issachar Street, I finally arrive at Throne Square. Memories of my first visit to the Throne Room come flooding back. Truly unforgettable was the all-powerful presence of God and Jesus Messiah, among so many angels. I'm so looking forward to spending more time there, and I expect each subsequent visit to be equally amazing.

As usual lots of people are entering and leaving the Throne Room, and for a moment I hesitate; I'm drawn to go inside. But I quickly remind myself that the reason I've come to the city centre is to discover more about Benjamin Street.

Weaving around several groups of eager worshippers, I make my way across the southern end of the shining, blue plaza. I follow the outer curve of the Throne Room's translucent, golden-yellow building until I pass the eastern entrance.

'Here's what I wanted to see,' I say to myself as I crouch down beside the foundation of the wall.

Water is flowing out from the base of the wall through a narrow opening, which is about fifteen centimetres high and just one metre wide. The rivulet is barely five centimetres deep and runs along a shallow streambed carved into the sapphire plaza.

One of many things that really surprised me on my first visit to the Throne Room was the sight of fresh water pouring out from under God's throne. The water flowed silently across the blue crystal floor, towards the eastern side of the building.

I'm not the only curious citizen to have been drawn to this location. A group of about twenty adults stand either side of the little stream, and are clearly fascinated by what they see. I can't help but overhear as they share their theories and question each other.

'Why is the stream here? Where does the water go? Isn't the eastern entrance the most important? Does Messiah use this entrance?

A short distance away, a small gathering of youths are casually chatting to each other, while standing with their feet half-submerged in the trickling water. I guess they are enjoying the feel of the refreshing water, as it runs around their bare feet.

Just as I pass the youths, one of the boys steps back and almost loses his balance. This makes them all laugh out loud, including the young man himself. I can't help but chuckle.

At the edge of the plaza, the flowing water tumbles gently down the steps. From here it forms a shallow stream just two metres wide. Slowly it begins its journey across the rest of the square and along its blue riverbed in the middle of the street. As I follow its progress I notice the inscription on the corner building - BENJAMIN STREET.

'So this is it, the street with the river,' I say to myself.

I'm particularly keen to see where the river leads, so I set off along Benjamin Street. My plan is simply to follow the course of the stream, by keeping close to the water's edge. On either side of the golden street, the tall buildings reflect the gently flowing river with dazzling effect.

Each structure stands four or five stories high and follows a familiar design. Narrow arched entrances give access from the street, and on every level there are rows of balustraded, viewing balconies. I love the different colours of crystal from which these beautiful buildings are made. There are blues, greens, aquamarine and gold, all perfectly blended together. Nothing looks out of place. On different floors, residents look out from their balconies. Dressed in their white robes they watch the busy street below. One lady even waves directly at me and smiles as I look up at her. Maybe she recognises me.

Far above the street, I observe more angels in flight; the sky is clear and tinged with green. Angels are always so occupied doing their work, travelling to important destinations. My life seems very relaxed compared to their hectic schedules.

As I follow the river, there are lots of people walking towards the city centre; some in groups, others on their own or accompanied by an angel. Several times I get smiles from the citizens I pass; I smile back with a nod of appreciation. Citizens frequently recognise their friends, and this adds to the strong sense of community. Everyone seems to be full of purpose and expectation.

The happy shouts of a group of young, excited children attract my attention. They chase each other across the street. Backwards and forwards, they dash through the shallow water, skilfully avoiding the adults. Small, wet footprints remain visible as droplets on the bright gold paving. The children come from different nations. I recognise some as African, others Asian along with a few white kids. I love the way they're all joining in the same game together, and clearly having such a great time. It brings a smile to my face, as I remember my own childhood of innocent fun; memories of happy family times. I think of my mum and dad, my younger brother Josh, and older sisters, Suzie and Sarah.

After following the river for a couple more blocks, I get a surprise. I spot someone I know. He's walking towards me among the crowds. I wave, hoping to attract him. He sees me, and quickly approaches me with a big grin.

'Hello Lucas, how are you?' I say, feeling really pleased to see him again.

We pause, briefly facing each other.

'I'm just off to the Library to do some reading,' he says enthusiastically. 'What about you, Jamie?'

'Well, I just want to see where the river leads,' I reply.

'Benjamin Street is a great area,' Lucas responds. 'When you've finished, feel free to come round to my apartment. Everyone around here knows where I live. I'll show you around the neighbourhood.'

'I'd love that,' I reply.

Lucas pats my shoulder and continues on his way. I'm still amazed at the way we both met. Although everyone is so helpful in heaven it's really good to make new friends, especially when you meet them again unexpectedly.

I'm quickly discovering that in heaven you're always meeting people you already know; as if by pure coincidence. In spite of the millions of citizens who live here, and the busy atmosphere of city life, you're more likely than not to meet someone you know. I now realise that such chance meetings are a special feature of life in the city. There's an overriding sense of always being in the right place at the right time. This is normal, and it makes me very happy and very much at peace. I'm also learning that no one can ever be late, nothing gets delayed and also you're never kept waiting. Imagine that - it's incredible. But then, this is heaven!

Further along the river, I see a group of women dancing and singing; some of them are shaking tambourines over their heads. A growing crowd of citizens has gathered to watch what's happening. I walk a bit faster until I reach the group of energetic performers and stand among the onlookers. Around thirty women, including a few young girls, are dancing beside the edge of the river.

They move swiftly in harmonious sequence, as their long hair flows behind them and their lavender robes swirl around. At times they raise their hands as an expression of praise, and then they sweep down low to the ground in adoration. Over and over they sing about God's victory over his enemy. I'm sure these are words I've read in the Bible.

'I will sing unto the Lord, for he has triumphed gloriously, the horse and rider fell into the sea.'

An older lady standing next to me, points to one of the leading dancers. I can't help hearing, as she speaks to her friend.

'Miriam is such an inspiration among the women.'

Her friend replies, 'Yes, I love to see the dancers, especially when they perform altogether in Praise Pavilion.'

I've already spotted the enormous, oval amphitheatre of Praise Pavilion just north of the Throne Room. Now I know for sure I must go there soon.

Then I think to myself, Miriam? Could this be Miriam, the Israelite, and the sister of Moses? I need an answer. So I turn to the ladies, smile and look them straight in the eyes.

I ask them, 'Excuse me ladies, did you mention the name Miriam? Is she the same Miriam who danced beside the waters of the Red Sea?'

With beaming smiles they roar with laughter, look at me and reply in unison, 'Of course she is.'

'Thank you, that's brilliant,' I say and continue to watch the dance with added interest.

I then ask the ladies, 'Do they dance regularly in the pavilion?'

'Oh yes, all the time', says the older lady. 'You must go and see them. These are just a few of the dancers. We hope to see you there soon, and will promise to look out for you. By the way, we are sisters, my name's Edith and my younger sister is called Ethel.'

'I will, yes I will,' I reply as they turn to leave and walk on, engaged in more conversation.

With renewed enthusiasm, I stand and watch the routine again with its inspired dance movements and rhythmic singing.

A united shout brings the dance to a sudden end. I clap my hands, along with all the other citizens who are applauding the dancers, and praising God for his victory.

As I think about Miriam, I'm bowled over by the thought of the generations going back thousands of years, who now occupy this fantastic city. Heaven is not only the place where God dwells, but also the celestial home for all of his people. I've already met Lucas and seen Nicodemus, now I've spotted Miriam.

'Who will I see next?' I ask myself.

Walking on a little further, I see the raised arch of a beautiful bridge crossing the river. This is at the junction where Benjamin Street meets one of the tree-lined avenues. The bridge itself is carved from white crystal, with a set of steps at either side providing an easy means of crossing. There's a name inscribed on the central span that reads MIRIAM BRIDGE.

'No surprise about that name,' I say to myself, having just seen the famous woman herself. I also quickly discover that the avenue is also named in her honour - Miriam Avenue.

Just as I reach the bridge I look twice. Guess who's there, sitting on the carved, crystal bench, and already waiting for me?

'Thaniel, what are you doing here?' I ask with surprise; knowing we are miles from the city centre.

'Oh, I heard you were heading this way,' he replies.

'It's great to see you again,' I respond.

Together we take the path under the bridge, with just enough head room to spare, and follow the course of the river. I do appreciate his friendship.

After a short distance, Thaniel makes a suggestion.

'Would you like to walk in the river, rather than just alongside? Walking in the river is an experience I know you'll love.'

'Okay, I'm game,' I say without any hesitation.

The river at this point is around three metres wide and still quite shallow. Together we step into the water, which is half-way up to our knees. The water is cool and refreshing; we begin to walk through the river.

'Have you seen the source of the river?' Thaniel asks.

'Yes, I have', I reply, adding with confidence, 'It's from God's throne isn't it? It flows out through the eastern wall.'

He explains, 'This is God's river of life. It not only brings life into all of heaven but also brings life to people on earth. You've already tasted this water while on earth. This is the same water that Jesus spoke about when he said, *Whoever drinks of the water I give him will never thirst again.*'

I tell Thaniel, 'I remember hearing from the pastor of my church about the gift of living water. Better still, I'll always remember the moment when I was filled with the Holy Spirit. I felt the gift of new life springing up, like a well of water inside me.'

I realise the water is getting deeper and it's already up to my knees. I'm starting to feel the gentle flow of the river around my legs, so I tuck the bottom of my robe up through my linen belt.

My eye catches an older couple, hand in hand, walking slowly alongside the river. They appear to be totally pre-occupied in their conversation and look so content. I think of Gramps and Grandma and their love for each other. It's just great that Christian couples become reunited for all eternity.

The street becomes much quieter and the large houses on either side are more spaced out. There are many leafy trees growing close to the river, some with ripe fruit hanging from the branches. Other trees are displaying soft pink and lilac blossom and heaven's sweet fragrance drifts over the river. Up ahead I watch reflections of the trees playing on the surface of the water and creating beautiful patterns.

We push on steadily, wading through the water, until we reach the next bridge at the crossroad. We take a short break and sit together on one of the crystal benches next to the bridge. I see this one's called RACHEL BRIDGE. Thaniel sees me looking at the carved inscription.

He says, 'You probably can already guess who Rachel is?

'I suppose this Rachel was Jacob's wife, the one he really loved and waited so long to marry?' I answer as I remember the story from the Bible.

'Yes, you're right. But not everyone realises this at first. Well done.' Thaniel compliments me.

He tells me, 'The avenues in heaven are a series of twelve circular routes that radiate out from the centre of the city. They cross each of the main highways that lead to Throne Square. These white arched bridges are found all the way along Benjamin Street. They enable anyone walking along the avenues to easily get from one side of the river to the other. Rachel herself lives in one of the apartments on this avenue, which is named in her honour. But it's over on the west side of the city near to the Banqueting Hall.'

Thaniel continues, 'Each of the twelve avenues is named after one of the women of faith from the first covenant between God and his people Israel. Starting from the city centre, the avenue names are as follows; Miriam, Rachel, Deborah, Ruth, Rebekah, Leah, Sarah, Rahab, Esther, Bathsheba, Naomi and Hannah.'

Either side of the bridge, there are two canals leading away from the river. They're just like the canals I've already seen, carved out of blue sapphire and with steep sides.

I ask Thaniel, 'Where do these canals go?'

Thaniel explains, 'You saw the canals when you first arrived in heaven; they run alongside each of the twelve avenues. Every canal distributes water to the thousands of small streams and fountains, which are found in every town and village. This continuous supply of pure water from the Throne Room is highly valued by citizens throughout the city.'

'That's so interesting, thanks. I guess I must have missed seeing the canals back at Miriam Bridge, probably just as you showed up,' I reply, as Thaniel smiles back wryly.

Then I remember reading in the Psalms, where King David wrote about *"a river, whose streams make glad the city of God"*.

We resume our wade through the deepening river, which is soon up to our waists. Our robes are drenched and progress is slow, even with the gentle current behind us.

I pluck up the courage and ask, 'Can we swim?'

'Yes, of course,' he answers immediately.

Without another word, we both plunge forward and dip right under the surface of the water, creating a small wave. Side by side we swim slowly, gently pushing the warm water back repeatedly with our hands and feet. My robe offers little resistance as I settle into my strokes and swim on for some distance. I feel energised. Heaven is such an incredible place. I look round to tell Thaniel how I feel. But he's gone - vanished again! Alone with my thoughts I continue to swim on through the water. I'm feeling so happy.

On both sides of the river, I begin to see mile after mile of rich green grass, with small areas of woodland in the distance. Then to my amazement, I glimpse hundreds of white horses galloping across the open parkland. It's such a beautiful sight that I stop swimming. I'm out of my depth now, so I tread water to stay upright and watch. I'm captivated as I wait for the horses to approach. They're just like the mature, white stallions I saw earlier in the chariot procession near the city centre. As they pass just a hundred metres away, the sound of their hooves on the soft grassy ground reverberates, sending ripples scudding across the surface of the river. A few moments later they are gone and calm returns.

Deciding it's time to get out of the river, I swim over to the bank. As soon as my feet touch the smooth river bed, I carefully make my way up the shallow bank and out of the water. Dripping wet, I walk across to the river bank and sit down on the lush green verge. The grass is immaculate, weed-free and barely a centimetre tall. There's a steady flow of citizens walking along Benjamin Street towards the city centre and I wonder if some are new arrivals. I think back to my first impressions of the city as I arrived.

The sound of splashing water alerts me to the sight of two young people swimming energetically in the river. Their heads are down and their arms pull and push under the water, with legs kicking alternatively. They swim quickly and have no time to notice me; I think they're in a race. What fun they're having.

My robe soon dries and I set off along the bank of the river until I reach an orchard. All the fruit looks delicious, and I recognise what I think are plums, peaches and rosy apples. I also catch sight of a beautiful walled garden nearby.

Leaving the river behind me, I follow a path through the grass to take a look at the garden. I pass through an apple-green crystal pergola, which forms the entrance. Once inside the view is stunning and the air is heavy with scent, reminding me of sweet honeysuckle.

The large rectangular garden is fully enclosed by a two-metre high wall, built with olive-green topaz. At the far end are rows of small trees full of different kinds of luscious fruit. The centrepiece is a beautiful crystal fountain. It's carved out of honey-gold crystal, which causes the flowing water to appear like liquid gold. I watch the water as it springs up about half a metre high, and then cascades down into a series of three bowls before filling the pool below. The garden is so peaceful and an absolute haven.

Surprisingly, there are only a few citizens around. There are three elderly people who are sitting on a bench and deep in conversation. Two young women, around my own age, pass by and smile. I smile back, and wonder how my friend Catherine is doing.

On my right hand side I see rows of vines supporting giant clusters of ripe, purple grapes. Over to my left the garden is laid out in a series of formal flowerbeds, with a dazzling display of bright colours. I select one of many garden seats, carved in the same honey-gold crystal as the fountain, and sit down to admire the garden in more detail.

As I watch the water constantly tumbling from the top of the nearby fountain and listen to the sprinkling water, I reflect back on my family life.

I remember my childhood fascination with the water fountain in our local park. I loved to look out for the golden Koi, swimming around between the large lily pads. I remember my dad chasing my brother Josh and I round and round the fountain. We also had lots of fun in the fenced play area with its slides, climbing frames and swings.

As memories come flooding back, I realise how much I miss my family and friends. Yet I have no sorrow or grief, and I do so hope they are not sad about me.

I think to myself, if only they knew how happy I am, and how astonishing heaven really is.

I'm pleased to know that Gramps and Grandma Minnie, my uncle and aunts are here with me. I'm also making some great new friends too, like Lucas and Thaniel.

A young man approaches me. I hadn't noticed him in the garden earlier.

'Can I sit beside you?' he asks in a friendly manner.

'Yes, of course,' I reply noticing his dark, Asian features.

'My name's Ishran,' he says, looking directly at me, with a smile mirrored in his deep brown eyes.

After a short pause he continues, 'I do love this garden; it's so tranquil. I find it a great place to think about things and to appreciate all we have in heaven.'

I reply, 'Well I'm Jamie, and it's my first visit to Benjamin Street and this garden. In fact, I'm fairly new to heaven.'

Ishran continues. 'I became a Christian when I was eighteen years old. It was through a friend I got to know in the city of Mumbai, India where I worked in marketing. My family lived in the suburb of Panvel and were Urdu speaking Sunni Muslims. When I told them about my new faith in Jesus as the Son of God, I was beaten by my dad. I was then forced to leave home and abandoned by my entire family. This was not unusual in my culture. I managed to share a small flat with another Christian friend in Mumbai, and attended the local fellowship church.'

'At just twenty-three years old I was kidnapped early one morning, while on my way to work and taken away in the back of a car. I was tortured and imprisoned by a gang of thugs, who claimed to be Hindu extremists. My wounds became badly infected, and I then got a fever while I was locked in my room. I died. Arriving at the gates of heaven was a truly wonderful experience, hearing those trumpets, seeing the city full of light and meeting the Lord himself.'

My eyes fill up with tears, as I hear Ishran's story. He's so full of joy and I really like him.

I respond, 'Ishran, let me tell you something about my own life. I grew up in a Christian family where we all went to church. In my late teens I began to realise I didn't know God in a personal way, like some of my friends did. I knew lots about the Bible, but in my heart there was something missing. I began to pray about this and read the Bible in a new way. I would underline verses that I thought were important, and then write the date in the margin. Several months later, at an Easter camp, I committed my life to God and promised to serve him for the rest of my life. This brought great peace into my life and I discovered a hunger for more of God's presence in my life. Soon afterwards, I was filled with the Holy Spirit and received the gift of praying in a heavenly language.'

Ishran nods gently as he carefully listens; watching me with barely a blink.

I share more, 'I went to Bath University to study architecture, and as a student I got involved in the Christian Union. We organised prayer meetings, outreaches and Bible studies. Soon after qualifying, I got a job with an architectural practice in Abingdon. It was a great time, especially when I started dating Catherine, my girlfriend. I lived at home with my parents and was busily involved in my local church.'

'But shortly after my twenty-seventh birthday I began to feel unwell with headaches, blurred vision and I began to lose weight. There were more tests at the hospital. The news was not good. I had leukaemia. My girlfriend and family were totally shocked, but they stayed very brave, and gave me all the love and support they could.'

'My church was fantastic. I had blood transfusions and many sessions of chemotherapy. They prayed and fasted for my healing, and the church leaders anointed me with oil in the name of the Lord. In spite of everything my faith remained strong even in my final days, which were hazy and confusing for much of time. I remember the smiles of my parents and family as I lay in bed, feeling very weak. I was so proud of them. I must have fallen asleep. The next thing I knew, I was walking through a heavy mist towards the city. And here I am in heaven!'

Ishran reaches out his hand, and briefly grips my forearm.

'I'm sure we'll become good friends,' he says.

'Jamie, where do you live?' asks Ishran.

'Oh, my apartment is just off Issachar Street, near to Rachel Avenue. What about you?' I respond.

'Well my place is near the junction of Simeon Street and Ruth Avenue,' Ishran answers.

We decide to leave the garden and follow the river back towards the city centre. Soon, we are exchanging stories about our experiences of heaven, and what we've discovered so far. We talk about the places we've been to and the people we've met - not forgetting our special angel friends. We also share ideas about what we are most looking forward to.

'I can't wait to visit Praise Pavilion?' I say.

'Me too,' says Ishran, 'Although I've already been there loads of times. The power of praise is massive and I just love everything that happens.'

We agree to go straight to Praise Pavilion and I can't wait. Ishran is a great guy. His love for God really touches me. I can so easily relate to him, even though we were born on different continents. He's already like a brother to me.

My visit to Benjamin Street has opened up so many wonderful surprises that I'm feeling absolutely great. I'm so glad that Gramps told me about it - or rather didn't tell me, but let me find out for myself.

Every part of heaven is filled with the life of God. It's a city that is eternal and all-powerful. This is the heart of God's kingdom - the kingdom he is establishing on the earth.

PRAISE PAVILLION

We step across the little stream, close to the eastern entrance to the Throne Room, and make our way across the shining, blue plaza. It's my very first visit to Praise Pavilion and my friend Ishran, who's been before, is taking me there. Since we met in the walled garden near Benjamin Street, I've had the feeling that we will become really good friends.

Leaving the plaza steps, at the north side of the square, we head up into Judah Street towards the sound of majestic music ahead. It's a really busy area, with thousands of people coming and going along the gleaming gold highway. Young and older people are all sharing the same wonderful sense of excitement; I can see groups of children eagerly chatting. Some citizens have already begun to join in with the songs of praise now echoing around the street. Meanwhile I try to picture what awaits us inside. All I know is that everything will be on a massive scale.

Towering sixty metres in front of us is the huge, oval amphitheatre with its red and white striped, onyx walls.

'It's a megastructure,' I announce.

Ishran explains, 'The pavilion is the largest single structure built in heaven and has no fewer than twelve entrances. It's the combined size of six football pitches, and the only building in heaven without a roof.'

Light reflects off the polished walls throwing a soft-pink hue over everyone's white robes. We pass two crowded entrances at the southern side, and walk on round to the middle entrance on the western side. It still looks busy here, but I guess Ishran has a favourite place he prefers.

'This way Jamie,' Ishran calls out, as he pulls firmly at my sleeve.

We quickly make our way towards a wide-arched entrance, and join a group of around thirty people as they slowly enter the pavilion. I notice many citizens are wearing their crowns for the occasion.

After walking through the illuminated passageway, we step out into a vast tiered stadium. The sound of singing reverberates across the arena and is almost deafening.

Ishran shouts to me, 'Up here.'

I just manage to see him, as he turns round and climbs up a tall flight of steps behind us. I follow after him, joining a queue of people going up in single file. To my right, there's a line of people making their way down. On either side, I see the long terraces with row after row filled with citizens; everyone looks so happy. Some folk are standing with arms raised high as they sing, while others simply sit and watch in amazement. Up we climb until we reach a second passage, only to repeat the ascent up a further flight of steps into the second tier. Ishran finally stops.

He says, 'We'll sit over there.' Turning right, I follow him past several people already seated in the same row, who offer us welcoming smiles. At last we find two vacant seats and sit down. We're sitting in one of the many rows of coral-coloured crystal benches with comfortable, curvy edges.

Praise Pavilion is packed with more than 200,000 people. I estimate the huge oval amphitheatre measures 200 metres across and around 350 metres wide. Below us, I can see hundreds of children sitting along the front rows of the lower level. Many young people are also gathered together in large groups.

Much of the loud singing we can hear is coming from the upper level, which is filled with thousands of angels. There are fabulous views of the angels standing on the opposite side of the arena; we can see them with arms raised and praising God. Their shining presence creates an added circle of light around the whole amphitheatre. Overhead the sky is golden with pale-red, aurora rays. The angels in flight seem to be unaware of the celebrations below, as they travel to and from their appointments.

For now, the vast central arena of the pavilion stands empty like a stage waiting for performers. The floor is laid out in apple-green quartz, and surrounded by a walkway of shining gold. Ishran leans toward me and points to the opposite side of the pavilion.

'Can you see the royal balcony in the middle over there? It's on the third level and carved out of ruby-red crystal,' he asks.

I nod and reply, 'Yes I can. It's just below the angels.'

'Well, keep watching,' Ishran adds, 'because when the trumpet sounds, Jesus will appear and take his place to preside over the whole gathering.'

More people are arriving and there are hardly any empty seats to be seen. The song of the angels ends on a long harmonious chord that trails away, leaving the sustained buzz of conversation. The atmosphere is charged and expectant.

A few moments later, a fanfare of trumpets sounds out triumphantly across the arena. The musical notes are repeated with rousing precision. I can see the golden glint of the long trumpets held up by around twenty angels stood in the upper terrace, which overlooks the royal balcony. Everyone immediately stands. We wait for Jesus to arrive.

All conversation is quickly hushed and silence falls across the whole pavilion. Every eye looks toward the royal box as a white, glowing haze begins to form. From within the glory cloud, Jesus the Messiah appears, with two cherubim standing on either side.

I can just make out that Jesus is wearing a gold crown and dressed in a dazzling white robe with a bright, golden sash across his chest. His right hand is lifted high, as if to acknowledge the huge crowd.

Loud shouts echo in unison like peals of thunder around the huge arena.

'King of kings and Lord of lords.'

As if rehearsed, Ishran and I join in.

'King of kings and Lord of lords... King of kings and Lord of lords.'

Jesus slowly lowers his raised hand and then sits on his balcony throne. Everyone else begins to be seated, creating a giant ripple effect around the pavilion. A great feeling of awesomeness descends on everyone, and a shiver goes down my spine.

I turn to Ishran and whisper, 'This is staggering!'

He looks at me with his dark eyes burning and says, 'Just wait and see'.

Another angelic fanfare blasts out across the pavilion.

Ishran says, 'Look over there at the Judah entrance.' As he points to our extreme left.

Through the arena's northern entrance, emerges a growing procession of musicians. They walk quickly toward us in rows along the golden walkway. They are wearing red and white striped robes with silver sashes, and some of them are wearing golden crowns. As they get nearer I recognise a variety of musical instruments are being carried. I can see trumpets, cornets and horns, along with flutes, violins and small harps. The orchestra assembles in an arc of seven rows directly below us on the crystal floor of the arena. Standing still, the men, women and young people face toward Jesus in the royal balcony opposite. All five hundred musicians then lift their instruments into position ready to play. There's no conductor to be seen.

The soft sound of the orchestra's hundred violins heralds the opening of a symphony of praise. Long, high notes of the strings float in unison like waves across the arena. From under the royal balcony, a line of little children come running, two by two. Dressed in deep-blue robes, they move quickly and silently to the centre of the arena to form a tight, swirling circle. Older children, also dressed in blue, quickly follow them; first in lines of four, then in eight and finally in rows of sixteen. This widening river of life forms a sea of movement centre-stage.

The flutes now take up the haunting tune as the violins sustain a shimmering sound, which seems to hover in the air with anticipation. As silent onlookers, we are startled by the awakening staccato of the orchestra's fifty trumpeters. In the sky above the pavilion, a throng of around 300 angels suddenly appears with dazzling effect, and slowly descends over the middle of the arena.

The horns now sound out the familiar melody, replacing the flutes. This added momentum causes the blue sea to change its shape. The children begin to lie down on the floor to form a solid circle of blue, as the descending angels spread out their robes over them to form a broad, white canopy.

Accompanied by the harps, the violins return to the main theme with majestic harmonies. More children, dressed this time in rich green robes, stream out from under the royal box. Some run right underneath the angelic canopy, and others gather around the edges of the blue sea. As the scene develops, the angels start to separate out allowing the first signs of green land to appear among the waters.

I turn to Ishran and ask, 'Where do these musicians and dancers come from? This is so beautiful.'

He replies, 'New musicians and dancers take part here each time the orchestra plays in the pavilion. There are thousands of musicians in heaven and I guess they come from towns and villages across the city.

Every local community has its own group of performers who take part in local celebrations. Praise squares are found in every neighbourhood, where hundreds gather together regularly to sing, dance and declare God's greatness. You've probably already heard them, even if you haven't seen them. '

I remember seeing the children singing and dancing close to my apartment.

Meanwhile, the rhythm of the melody quickens and the music of the violins rises and falls repeatedly. The angels who created the canopy commence their slow ascent above the pavilion, and eventually disappear from view. More children run from the eastern entrance, wearing an array of vivid colours, to join the drama unfolding at the centre of the arena. Among the mass of green and blue colour there now appear flashes of yellow, scarlet, turquoise and emerald.

The music becomes playful and lively, as horns and flutes rejoin the orchestra to create a dynamic crescendo. The young dancers begin to leap about, and raise their hands while spinning around, to reveal a scene that's full of life and motion.

The orchestra plays another fanfare, firstly by the horns, then echoed by the cornets and finally by the trumpets. As the music reaches its climax, a line of men and women dancers appear from the western entrance below us. Dressed in their long white robes, they run forward holding hands, and encircle the main group of younger dancers. The long-held notes of the trumpets provide a signal to the whole cast. They all turn toward Jesus in the royal box, and respectfully kneel and bow down. Everyone in the pavilion erupts in a long period of praise with shouts, whistles and clapping, to add their thankfulness to God as Creator.

Although choked with emotion and with tears in my eyes, I feel elated. I look at Ishran, and watch as the tears roll down his dark brown cheeks. More than the beautiful music and expressive dance; it's the very atmosphere of heaven that's so compelling. The presence of the Lord is felt everywhere. Quietness gradually descends on the pavilion. The children slowly lie down, in a decorative pattern of green and blue, before the sound of violins fills the air again.

At exactly the same moment, from the north, east, south and west of the arena emerge scores of adult dancers dressed in plain white robes. Using the open spaces around the arena, they glide forward in long curving lines, lifting their arms with grace and charm. As the tune of the strings quickens its pace, each of the four lines of dancers form a series of twelve circles, and dance with enfolding movements of great fluidity. From within each circle, a lead dancer moves to the centre and pirouettes with startling poise, once, twice and three times.

In the middle of the arena, the older children slowly rise from the ground. They begin their tip-toe routine, as they delicately circle around the resting infants a short distance away. Then as the cornets and horns play their close harmonies, the curled-up infants slowly stretch their limbs and arise into life. They too start to push themselves forward, in a clockwise direction, by extending their young legs with synchronized movements.

The whole orchestra joins together in a loud finale, and the whole troupe of dancers regroups to face Messiah Jesus. They stand in a perfect square with the adults at the back and the children in front. Suddenly, high in the upper terrace the angel choir breaks forth into thunderous song.

'Hallelujah, hallelujah,' they sing with notes loud and long.

The trumpets echo the melody as Ishran and I, along with everyone else, begin to join in a great hymn of praise. Lifting their hands in praise, all the dancers advance toward the royal box. They take three diagonal paces to the right and then with three similar paces, they move to the left.

Ishran and I continue to sing out with loud abandonment, along with everyone else around us. The angels keep on singing and the high notes of the tenors ring out loudly with adoration. My heart is full and overflowing with love for Jesus. I'm singing directly to my Saviour, face to face. It's a truly wonderful experience to sing out so freely, and with such deep-felt desire. This is truly heavenly harmony. It's far greater than any earthly choir or church gathering I've ever known.

Clusters of flags appear simultaneously at all twelve of the pavilion's entrances, and each group is displayed in a different colour. The two-metre square banners are raised high on golden poles and held by white-robed standard bearers.

Ishran tells me, 'Each set of flags represent the colours of the twelve precious foundation stones located at the city gates.'

In the far left corner of the north stand I see crimson red flags, and then at the main north entrance are flags with red and white stripes. At the third northern entrance is a group of emerald colours. Opposite us are first the pure white flags and under the royal box, the sapphire emblems, and then a set of dark green flags.

Emerging from the far corner at the southern side of the arena is a group of yellow flags, and then turquoise banners in the middle followed by some in olive-green. Finally the standards in front of us, from the right hand side are apple-green, then lavender and finally, burgundy. The scene is set and the angelic singing ends.

A short fanfare, by the trumpet section below us, echoes around the pavilion and acts as a cue to the flag carriers. Led by the brass section, the orchestra commences its military-style music with a steady rhythm. From all twelve entrances the flags are ceremonially marched forward, at intervals of around ten metres between each one. Each flag is lifted high and carried towards the 1000 dancers at the centre of the arena. At the halfway point, each line of flag carriers merges to create one large square, which measures about 120 metres across. The flags fly side by side, with a gap between each one of around three metres.

Everyone turns to face Messiah in the royal box. Matching the colours of their respective entrances, the flag-bearers stand like sentinels and hold up their banners until the music ends. Every flag is then lowered to the ground as an act of homage to the Lord Jesus. After several moments of quietness the flags are lifted high once again.

From the western entrance beneath us appears a female dancer with thick, flowing black hair. Dressed in a lavender robe, she skips and twirls as she passes the orchestra and repeatedly raises her arms up high. Scores more dancers follow her and wave their jingling tambourines. It dawns on me that the woman who leads them must be Miriam.

Applause and cheering echo across the arena. For a brief moment I think about Edith and Ethel, the two elderly sisters I met, when I first saw Miriam in Benjamin Street. I look around and wonder if they are somewhere in the vast crowd.

The group of dancers move between the fluttering flags, and toward the main assembly in the centre of the arena. The steady beat of the tambourines can now be clearly heard. The rhythm is matched by a new melody flowing from the flutes, which sounds to me rather like an Irish jig. A short series of notes rises and falls, only to be repeated, and then the joyful tune is played again at a higher pitch. Miriam and her timbrel-waving dancers reach the main group, who all begin to join the same dance with perfect footwork and face towards Messiah Jesus.

The flutes are joined by the whole orchestra, including brass and strings, and the dance immediately takes on a whole new dimension. I notice many of the children on the front rows and youths in the terraces are beginning to spill out into empty spaces around the arena, to join the main dancers. They are quickly followed by streams of people, and very soon thousands are finding room to join the dance. The number of people in the main arena now spreads well beyond the flag carriers, who hold their positions. The atmosphere is exuberant and dynamic. I look to Ishran, he looks back at me. Without saying a word, we both move out along the row and join the line of citizens walking down the steps of the terrace.

By the time we reach the arena it's getting quite full. We pass the full-on sound of the orchestra and join in the main assembly. Everyone down here is dancing before the Lord, and this releases a great feeling of joy. I've never danced like this before. My cousin once told me that I had two left feet - but that was back on earth. In heaven this dance is exhilarating!

The orchestra picks up the pace and everyone in the arena is joining in, leaping, jumping and twirling around. Even the flags are now being waved from side to side. As I look back, I see lots of people in the terraces who are on their feet and clapping in time with the music. A few feet away, I suddenly recognise two people who I know very well. Its Gramps and Grandma, who are dancing with a young woman with their arms locked together; they move backwards and forwards, again and again.

'Gramps, Grandma,' I call out excitedly.

They both see me and I skip across to them. They introduce me to Karen, my niece who's dressed as a member of the dance troupe. I'm simply stunned at the sight of Karen in her dance costume, not because of the outfit, but to see her no longer confined to her wheelchair and looking so well. I hold Karen in my arms and am unable to prevent the tears that run down my cheeks.

All four of us join hands and dance in a small circle to the sound of the music. Gramps takes much delight in frequently deciding to switch the direction of our dance. This is a wonderful experience and one I could never have imagined on earth.

The music softens and the dance pace slows. Three more people join themselves to our circle, and all around us I see people forming more circles. Adults, youth and children all taking part - no one is left out. While dancing around I spot two more people I know; they have both joined a circle nearby. It's my good friends Lucas and his friend Nick from the Library.

I shout across to them, 'Hi Lucas, Hi Nick.'

They both see me and shout back a quick, 'Hello Jamie,' before their dance circle turns away.

Eventually the music ends, leaving the gentle sound of angelic voices wafting across the pavilion. Hand slips from hand as the circles finally end. Some people start to make their way back to their benches, while others either stand or kneel on the ground. Gramps, Grandma Minnie and Karen return to their seats.

Right next to me, two little dancing boys wearing those lovely blue robes are knelt down together side by side, their eyes are wide open and their faces lifted up towards the Lord. It doesn't seem to matter to them that their view is mostly obstructed by the hundreds of adults moving around. Their young faces are glorious and radiant.

I feel a tap on my back and look round to see Ishran - he's all smiles. We hug each other for a moment, and then begin to quietly thank God for all his goodness. Before long, we're both on our knees before the Lord. There are not enough words to express the love I feel in my heart toward Messiah Jesus.

After some time, I realise most people have returned to their seats and only a few of us remain in the arena. The song of the angels continues to drift around the pavilion.

'Ishran, let's go back,' I suggest.

He nods his agreement. We stand up and return all the way up to the second level.

By the time we're back in our places, the atmosphere has changed, and there's a steady drone of conversation around the amphitheatre. A brief glint, from raised golden trumpets across the arena, catches my eye. Three victorious fanfare blasts follow.

From the southern entrance enters another procession of people, who are dressed in white robes and wearing purple sashes with golden crowns on their heads. They walk towards us in pairs along the gleaming walkway and are followed by a much larger group of citizens, including older people, youths and even a few children. They advance in rows of five, wearing white robes with golden sashes and all of them have crowns upon their heads. The audience begin to cheer, wave and clap as the whole procession arrives in the pavilion. In the middle of the arena, the flag bearers begin to sway their colourful flags once again.

I ask Ishran, 'Who are these people? Are they important?'

Ishran replies, 'These are citizens who are taking part in the honours procession. It takes place all the time.'

I interrupt, 'But who are those men in front? They look familiar.'

'Oh, they are the twenty-four honourable elders, who sit before God's throne. They always lead the procession,' explains Ishran. 'The people following them have just received their crowns. It's the custom to parade directly from the Hall of Honours to Praise Pavilion and to bring their honour to the Lord. You'll visit the Hall of Honours soon for yourself. It's a wonderful experience and one you'll never forget.'

The procession passes by in front of us, and I notice the marchers are wearing different crowns. Some are even wearing two or three crowns. I guess I'll find out why there are different crowns later on. As they arrive at the section of walkway directly in front of Messiah Jesus, they stop to form lines and turn to face him. Finally, the whole company reaches the eastern side. I watch closely as they carefully remove their shining crowns and lay them down in rows, as an act of devotion before the Lord. Together with the elders, they all kneel down on the arena floor and wait before the Lord. The flags are held still, and silence once again fills the pavilion. After quite some time, I watch as the glory cloud around the royal box gradually thickens, and Jesus and the two cherubim disappear from view. Everyone remains perfectly still and a remarkable peace rests over the whole pavilion.

Eventually, the faint sound of music arises from the orchestra, as the harps produce the rise and fall of many cadenzas. The flutes begin to softly repeat the tune we heard when the children first arrived. The pace is relaxed and reassuring. People around us start to stand up and move along the rows towards the steps. I realise my first visit to Praise Pavilion is coming to an end. Even before we leave, I can't wait to come back. I've loved every moment of it and especially the opportunity to offer my own praise and thanks to Messiah Jesus.

'Thanks so much, Ishran for bringing me here. It's been superb and way beyond anything I expected. I'm definitely coming back here soon.'

He replies, 'Yes, it's one of the many places in heaven I love. Each time I come here, it's as though it's just the first time. It really is impossible not to love Praise Pavilion.'

We get up to go and pass several people still sat in our row. As we make our way down through the terraces, more people are climbing up the steps in preparation for the next celebration. They will be glad there's plenty of space.

Finally, we leave the pavilion and make our way back to our different apartments. On reaching Throne Square, I say my goodbyes to Ishran who disappears off toward Benjamin Street, while I head straight for

Issachar Street and my long walk home. With so many incredible memories, I've plenty to think about.

Someone behind me calls my name.

'Jamie, over here.' It's Gramps calling me and he's with Grandma Minnie and Karen.

The four of us walk along the highway and share our best moments of Praise Pavilion. Karen talks about her joy of serving God in dance, having spent all her life on earth with major disability. Her life has been transformed in so many ways, for all eternity.

I say to Gramps, 'Praise in the pavilion never comes to an end. Eternity gives everyone plenty of time to take part.'

As a newly arrived citizen, I'm just starting to appreciate the difference eternity makes.

ABOUT TIME

I've arranged to meet up with Thaniel beside the canal at Rachel Avenue, so I'm taking the familiar route along Issachar Street. I've something on my mind.

Ever since I was a child, one of the things I've always loved to see is a sunset. This was especially true, when seen from either high up on a hill in the Cotswolds, or out across the open sea. Whenever I watched the sun setting, I always thanked God for the beauty of his creation as another day slowly ended. Here in heaven, there are no sunsets or sunrises, because there's no need for either a sun or a moon. Heaven has been designed with its very own source of light, generated by God's presence. Everything created here radiates with eternal light; the angels, the pearl gates, the crystal buildings, golden highways, streams and fountains, plants and trees. There's no place for darkness or even shadows. Daytime has a whole new meaning in heaven.

Time, as I previously knew it, was measured by the regular movements within the solar system. It was yearly duration of the earth's orbit as it travelled around the sun. The journey of the moon around the earth determined the lunar month. Every day, the earth completed a full rotation on its axis. Using these regular intervals every civilization was able to decide how years, months, days and hours were determined. The ancient Hebrews proclaimed the start each month at the exact rising of each new moon. Weeks, ending with the Sabbath day, came directly from the story of creation! In the modern era of atomic clocks, time also became measurable in nanoseconds - a billionth of a second.

Across the continents of the world, time varied across the different time zones, which followed the turning of the earth as it faced the sun. On earth everyone understood the importance of time, and from an early age we quickly learned how time worked. This allowed us to agree the time to meet up and do things, the times we arrived and left our work, and the time we met together as church. Although sometimes I wondered if the pastor forgot all about time while he was preaching!

As humans we also needed regular breaks to rest and sleep. Most importantly, our days as mortals on earth were also numbered; very few people lived beyond 100 years. So we tried to make time productive. As people got older they began to make efforts to stay 'young' and to keep healthy. We worked hard to fulfil our dreams and appreciated the time we spent with our family and friends. Time on earth was valued because it was always going to be limited; there were only so many hours each day.

Heaven is totally different. Here, there are no mornings and certainly no evenings, no months and no years - time has vanished into eternity. This is the eternal dwelling place, where our Heavenly Father lives. This is where the angels reside and from where Jesus, the Son of God came to earth as a baby. It's also where Jesus returned to prepare a place for us, with the promise of eternal life.

Just as I reach the canal, I see Thaniel already sat waiting for me on the wall of the bridge.

'Hi Thaniel,' I say, as I approach him.

We briefly embrace each other and sit down on the low wall. Thaniel, my guardian angel since childhood, knows me very well and I'm gradually getting to know him. So I come straight out with my question.

'Thaniel, would you please explain to me what eternity is about? I've been so used to time on earth that I find it hard to understand how time works in heaven.'

Thaniel pauses for a few moments and then says, 'Jamie, let's take a walk by the canal and I'll try and explain more about time in eternity.'

We both head off along the bank of the canal next to Rachel Avenue.

Thaniel says, 'As you already know, heaven has been designed and created by God as an eternal city. It was created perfect and complete; a city to last forever. It looks as sparkling new as the moment it was first created - as if no time has passed. Heaven's deep crystal foundations, the towering walls and magnificent structures you've already seen are everlasting. They can't crumble, or deteriorate, and will never need to be repaired. Heaven is indestructible. The golden highways never become worn down by the constant movement of millions of people who use them. Each object in heaven lasts for all eternity; the musical instruments, the flags, robes, scrolls and even the reed pens. Nothing needs to be discarded and there's never been a malfunction because everything is faultless.'

He continues, 'At some point in the future, after the Great Judgement, the whole city will be relocated to a new earth. The city will be known as the New Jerusalem. It will be the residency of every citizen, all the angels and God himself. Everything that has been built here in heaven will be established on earth.'

'So, does heaven have a past, as well as a future?' I ask Thaniel.

'Yes, God created heaven as an eternal city, before the earth, the solar system and the universe. Heaven was built before time began. God's kingdom is beyond time, and the life we now share together lasts forever.' Thaniel replies.

After following the canal for some distance, we take a turn and follow one of the many streams, which are fed with fresh water from the canal. Along the banks of the stream are clusters of flowers in bloom. They look rather like spring crocuses, and appear in many different colour combinations.

Thaniel sees my interest and continues our conversation.

'Even the flowers are eternal, they cannot die. In heaven, there's no soil, no decomposition and no muddy earth. Every flower shares eternity.

Whenever you pick a flower, in moments a new one will appear. When you take flowers back to your apartment, they always keep their colour and shape. Here nothing fades or even wilts.'

While watching the light playing on the clear crystal stream, I'm alerted by the sound of children singing nearby. I look across and see around thirty children, sat down in a flowery meadow, singing a song of praise. Two angels playing small harps are sat with them and teaching them to sing in two-part harmony.

'Yes Jesus loves me, yes Jesus loves me.'

Their young voices sound so sweet and perfectly in tune with the chords being strummed on the harps.

Thaniel says, 'Look at those children, they will never grow old, they'll stay young forever. They get looked after so well by the angels, with help from some of the young people. A few of them arrived with their parents and others will soon be reunited with their dad or mum. In heaven, all these little ones have clear speech from a very early age. They also have clever minds with unbelievable memories and wonderful personalities. No children are shy, although some are a little quieter by temperament. There are no squinty eyes, no missing teeth, no runny noses, and no grubby knees. Neither is there learning disability, physical disability, Down's syndrome or mental illness. All these little ones are wonderfully perfect and they are truly happy.'

I think of my niece, Karen, and the transformation of her life in heaven.

I can finally accept that in heaven our ages are fixed for eternity. No-one needs to grow older. There are no birthdays! But there's plenty to celebrate - we've stepped out of time and into eternity.

I think about Gramps and Grandma Minnie. Back on earth, they used to have problems with stiff joints, aches and pains. Gramps used a walking stick when going outdoors, and my grandma had to take medication to control her high blood pressure. Grandma also used to wear glasses to help her read. I remember them looking old and frail. But now, even though they are old, they are so full of life, with boundless energy and always in good health. Remembering the time when we danced together in Praise Pavilion brings a smile to my face.

With the meadow behind us, the stream passes between some trees in full leaf and the water glistens with a dappled light. Many of the trees have huge blossoms in a variety of colours and look rather like magnificent magnolias. There are shades of pink, white, orange and even blue. A sweet perfume hangs in the air.

In terms of height, the trees seem to vary from just two metres to around ten metres. Even the bark, which gilds the trunk and branches of each tree, appears in a range of different shades; bright silver, copper-red and burnished bronze. The leaves also vary in terms of colour and shape; some are broad and golden-yellow, others are heart-shaped and emerald-green, and there are also slim, red ones. My greatest surprise is that not a single leaf has fallen on the carpet of fresh green grass below.

I ask Thaniel, 'If the trees are eternal then how big do they grow?

He answers me with a chuckle, 'But the trees never grow larger. They were created this size and the branches remain the same length. They simply live and form these lovely flowers and soft, fine leaves. In heaven the plants and trees have life within them, so they don't need nutrients to help them grow. There's no autumn and no springtime - the seasons of seedtime and harvest are only found on earth. The trees in heaven are like the evergreens on earth; they never shed their leaves.'

He adds, 'Many trees produce fruit and because they are self-pollinating there's no need for insects to transform blossom into harvest. Whenever fruit is picked from the branches, the tree simply produces more. Heaven's fruit never falls to the ground, and when it's picked it stays ripe and fresh forever.'

'Thaniel, you are such a help to me. Thank you so much. I really like the way you explain things so simply.' I reply with an appreciative smile.

Thaniel says, 'Well, I better be getting back as there's something else I must do. So, why don't you just follow the stream through the trees? I'm sure you'll find your own way back.'

'I'll do that,' I reply, as he turns back toward the canal.

I follow the stream through the woods and emerge close to a small village. In the pretty square, there are some excited children playing a chasing game and lots of people are sitting around. I notice a young woman with ringlets of fair hair, sitting with her back to me. She's sat on one of the crystal benches facing the village fountain. As I get closer, I recognise her and stand just behind her.

'Hello,' I say, in a quiet voice.

She turns round, and gives me a beautiful smile of recognition.

'Hi there, how are you doing? Haven't I seen you before?' she asks me.

Immediately I recognise her US accent. I join her on the bench and introduce myself.

'Hello, my name's Jamie. I remember seeing you at the Issachar Gate. We arrived in heaven at the same time.'

'Hi Jamie, yes, I did arrive in heaven at the Issachar Gate, but I don't recall noticing you there. It all seemed so unreal at first, but my guardian angel has been amazing,' she says softly.

I respond, 'It was incredibly different for me too, until I began to adapt to life here. I'm now having an unbelievable time with so many great places to see. There's also so much to do in the city. I'm making lots of new friends and getting to know Thaniel, my guardian angel.'

She laughs at the mention of Thaniel. I'm unsure whether she's amused at his name or the thought of me with the angel.

'My name's Hannah,' she tells me. 'I'm from Chicago and was studying performing arts at high school in Lincoln Park. I also sang in the church youth choir and loved to play the flute.'

I seize the moment, 'Have you been to Praise Pavilion yet?'

She replies, 'No, not yet, but I'm so looking forward to going. Some of the musicians, who take part in the pavilion orchestra, told me all about the fabulous music and dancing.'

I say, 'Well, I've been to the pavilion just once. I can't wait to get back.'

Hannah nods and smiles again.

I ask her, 'What did you think about meeting God in the Throne Room? Isn't it just a magnificent place? When I stood before Almighty God and Jesus Messiah for the first time, it was a most amazing experience. Just as the day I became a believer was life-changing, so my first encounter with the risen Lord was totally transforming. To see the Lord of creation with my very own eyes felt like miracle in itself.'

Hannah replies in her sweet voice, 'I've been to the Throne Room twice already and each time I wanted to stay forever.'

After a thoughtful pause she continues, 'To be in the presence of God and to feel the power of his love flowing all over me was incredible. I've been truly at peace ever since. I cried so much when I saw Jesus for the first time - especially when I looked at the scars on his hands and feet.'

I respond. 'Well, I've only been once, but it was much the same for me. Having suffered a lot, both physically and emotionally, during my illness on earth I knew I was completely healed.'

'What happened?' Hannah asks. She looks directly at me; her caring heart shines through her pale blue eyes.

I tell her, 'I was diagnosed with cancer and had treatment in hospital over several months. But it in the end it was too late, and the doctors were unable to save me. My family were wonderful and prayed for me all the time, as did my church in the UK.'

'How about you, Hannah?' I ask, sensing she wants to tell me more about herself.

Hannah looks straight ahead at the sparkling fountain, and after a brief silence she tells me something of her own story.

She explains in a slow, quiet voice. 'I was returning home from church late one Sunday night, and was a passenger in the back seat of my friend's automobile. All I remember is the bright lights in my eyes, and the sudden impact of the smash. Next thing I know, I'm walking alone through the mist in the direction of the light and wearing this robe.'

As I turn toward Hannah I see an angel sitting on her left hand side. Angels are always around at the perfect moment. This angel looks rather like Thaniel. Knowing the angel is now sitting beside her, Hannah turns to me.

'Oh, this is Jediah,' she says, with a little gesture of her hand towards him. 'He's always showing up.'

She smiles at Jediah and says 'You're my special angel aren't you Jediah? My chaperone.'

Jediah says, 'Hannah, I'm just doing the job I love.'

'Hi Jediah,' I say, as I lean towards him.

He smiles back and waves his hand.

I ask Jediah, 'Do you know Thaniel, my guardian angel?'

He replies, 'Thaniel? Oh yes, we've known each other a very long time and have often served God together.'

Turning back to me, Hannah says, 'Jediah has told me that God has called me to serve him in heaven, rather than on earth. I am to use my gifts for eternity.'

'Hannah, that is so special. I'm so pleased for you,' I respond.

The concept of serving God in eternity really makes me think, and I wonder to myself if this is something I need to consider.

We all sit and watch the endless cascade of water from the fountain, and then Hannah tells me more about herself.

'Since the age of eight, when I attended my first children's camp in Mishawaka, Indiana, I knew I wanted to serve God. That's when I became a Christian. There's no greater joy than living for the kingdom of God,' she says smiling.

I nod in agreement and say, 'And to think, we have all of eternity to love God and serve him.'

I feel it's time to move on, so I say, 'I've really enjoyed talking with you, Hannah. I had better be going. I'm sure we'll meet up again.'

'Bye Jediah.'

As I get up, Hannah grins and waves her hand toward me. I walk on through the village and decide to leave the stream behind me and take a small path, which leads up to the grassy hills.

A verse from the Bible comes to mind and I can't get it out of my mind. I begin to repeat it in a whisper.

'One day with the Lord is like thousand years and a thousand years is like one day.'

I wonder to myself if this is a clue as to how time works in heaven. A millennium is a long time from an earthly point of view. Does this give me an idea of eternity? If there were days in heaven, then those days would be extremely long. Doing the maths I reckon that one day with the Lord would be equal to 365,000 days!

What these numbers suggest to me is that events in heaven can either last a very long time or take place in an instant of time. There's no way of knowing how long something lasts, whether it's a conversation, a song of praise, a meal or a journey. Imagine how brief is a 365 thousandth of a day. It sounds to me rather like the twinkling of an eye. When I think about the time it takes angels to travel on missions between heaven and earth; it frequently happens in a split second.

I remember one sunny morning, when I was driving my car along the dual carriageway near my home. A truck and trailer pulled out in front of me and there was a high speed collision. The sudden impact flipped my car 360 degrees, so it landed the right way up, but with the rear end of the vehicle resting on top of the central crash barrier. The car was written off by the insurers, but I stepped out without a bruise or a scratch. Immediately, I knew my unseen guardian angel, who I now know to be Thaniel, was instantly there to preserve my life. It was as though the angel had picked up the car and placed it down again. I also remember God immediately saying to me that he had unfinished work for me to do.

Time in heaven is both instant and also endless. Even if there was a single day in this city, it would appear to last forever. There's no need for sleep, so there are no bedrooms. I always have endless amounts of energy and am able to walk long distances without feeling tired. Walking up into the hills takes no effort. There's no exhaustion or sore blisters on my bare feet!

I look up, as another herd of horses are running free near the top of the hill. There are hundreds of white stallions, like the ones I saw beside the river in Benjamin Street. Their manes and tails fly in the breeze as they speed along. It occurs to me that even the horses in heaven live forever.

They never grow old, become sick or die. They were created in heaven by God to live in eternity and to serve his purposes.

I wonder to myself, if some of these horses were among those seen by Elijah. In a vision, the prophet and his young servant saw thousands of heavenly horses and chariots of fire. They had been sent to help him while he was trapped, with his life in danger, during a siege in a town called Dothan.

The longer I'm in heaven, the more I feel as if time somehow fast-forwards itself. This happens when I'm travelling around the city. Sometimes, without explanation, I suddenly find myself either at or very near to my destination. I'm unable to recall the specific details of the journey, what I saw or who I met. It's as though I was transported in an instant.

Although I must admit, sometimes I experienced this phenomenon during my earthly life. It would occur when travelling either with friends on a long journey, or even on my own along a route I took frequently. There was a sense of suddenly arriving and being unable to remember the journey.

Reaching the top of the hill I take a look around me. I gaze back towards the village in front of the woods, and see the stream sparkling in the light. In the distance I can also see the city centre and its tall distinctive buildings shining like jewels. I sit down to think about my time in heaven.

I make a fascinating discovery as I consider the way things happen in heaven. It's the realisation that in heaven the timing of everything is absolutely perfect. Ever since I arrived here, there's been a whole series of events that have taken place. I'm thinking about the people who I've met on different occasions. Then there are all those outstanding places I've visited during my travels around the city. I'm truly convinced that flawless timing is an expression of God's kingdom.

When I visited the Throne Room and experienced the presence of God, along with many thousands of other people, the place was full but not overcrowded. There were no long queues of citizens having to wait outside. No one was left disappointed because the place was full. Then there was the time Ishran and I went to Praise Pavilion. Yes, it was busy and the amphitheatre was packed, but not congested. When we found our seats, it just seemed as if our places were reserved. There are also the times when I've met different people, like Lucas in the Library, Ishran in the garden or Hannah, who I've just been talking to. Even Thaniel seems to show up at just the right time - not to mention his vanishing tricks!

In heaven, there's no need to be aware of time; as if hours and minutes really mattered. There's no rush to get home before its dark, no panic to get to the praise rehearsal in time. You can't even fix a special time to meet a friend. It just happens - at the right time.

On earth, most people are controlled by time. My own life, as an architect, was organised by the day and the hour; the schedule dominated my life. Time counted and appeared to be in short supply, even when things went well. During my last weeks on earth, time became critical - there was little of it left.

What a contrast in heaven where everything is eternal. I know it sounds like a cliché, but life here in the city is like a day that never ends. It's an everlasting life, continually filled with great experiences and joy-filled moments. There's never a rush to be on time and it's impossible to be late. You're never left waiting, with a sense of time anxiously slipping by. There are no missed appointments. My arrival in heaven looked as though it had been expected, with Thaniel assigned to meet me. My apartment was all furnished for me to move in, and even Gramps and Grandma Minnie didn't appear that surprised to see me.

While I was in the Throne Room, Jesus looked straight at me, and in that very moment I felt as if he had arranged the perfect time for me to meet him. I knew that the Lord had called me from time into eternity.

I remember when the pastor of my church spoke about God's timing, in one of his Sunday sermons. He said that God moves in mysterious ways, but he's never late to meet our needs even though it's often at the eleventh hour.

As a Christian I tried to trust God's timing, but didn't find it easy. Looking back on my life, I made too big a deal about time, as if it was my time. I wish I'd better understood the prayer Jesus taught us to say. If only my life on earth had been as it is in heaven.

Grandma Minnie often used the quaint expression 'serendipity' to describe those rare moments, when timings on earth just seemed to be perfect.

I wonder, 'Can there be divine coincidences?

I knew some people who used to say there were no mere coincidences with God. Serendipity seems to describe the feeling I frequently get in heaven, when all things work together so remarkably well.

Now, I hardly ever think about what awaits me in the future. The present moment fully occupies my heart and mind; there seems no reason to consider things still to come. No one ever talks about tomorrow. Now I understand why Jesus taught his followers to live on one day at a time. He was giving them a taste of the kingdom of heaven, while they lived on earth.

Unexpectedly, I notice that the view of the city has disappeared and that a veiled mist has settled on the hill around where I'm sitting. It's hard to describe, but I suddenly get the feeling that I'm no longer alone. Slowly, I turn my head to look behind me. I can't believe my eyes. It's Jesus Messiah and he's sat on a crystal ledge just two metres away.

'Lord!' I say as I turn right round to face him, 'You're here too!'

'Yes, Jamie, it's me,' he answers. 'I wanted a quiet place to meet with you.' He pauses.

'Tell me, what is it like to see all the things that were hidden from view on earth? To enter my Throne Room and to worship me and my Father? To bring your celebration before me in the pavilion? What is it like?'

'Lord, it's so good. It's amazing to be here,' I respond. 'To be with you and to share in your kingdom. I now live in a realm that is filled with eternal life and a place that you have prepared for me.'

Jesus says, 'Jamie, you have entered the place I prepared for you. But I think you already know that this place is far greater than your apartment - though I hope you like it. Your room in heaven is wherever you find yourself. It's your place in the Throne Room, your room in the Library, your seat at Praise Pavilion, your pew in the Hall of Honours or your table at the Banqueting Hall. Your place is in the village square, down by the canal, or up here in the hills. Your place is where I am. In my Father's house are many rooms; plenty of places to discover, different streets to walk along, gardens to admire and fields to explore. Make yourself at home. This is the place where you belong.'

As Jesus talks with me I feel totally at ease in his presence. These are intimate moments, as love pours from his eyes and his words are spoken with great reassurance. Divine life radiates from him and totally surrounds me.

Then Jesus looks deeply at me and says, 'I have also called you to a place where you will be further equipped to serve me. You will gain much understanding about my designs and plans for the future. When the earth is restored, I want you to help build my kingdom. You will join many others who will make decisions and take responsibility in the coming age.'

The power of his word resonates through my whole being as if it was being inscribed on the foundation stone of my heart. Fresh light fills my mind as this revelation of my role in eternity is absorbed. I'm filled with such peace and a great awareness of God's goodness and love.

'Lord, I accept your plan and purpose for my life. I love you Jesus.' Tears roll down my cheeks.

Jesus gets up and moves towards me. I also stand and we embrace each other. I feel the steady beat of his heart, my resurrected Lord. His arms hold me firmly and he kisses my wet cheek.

'I love you Jamie,' he whispers.

Slowly, Jesus steps back and without another word being spoken, I watch as the mist envelops him until he's gone from sight. I turn around and the view of the city is restored. I face the distant buildings but all I see before me is a vision of the face of Jesus. I think I will now see many things differently.

I find myself walking along the canal and approaching the bridge on Issachar Street. I've no recollection of walking back through the village or even following the stream through the woods. Either I've been wandering along deep in thought, or maybe I've just experienced heaven's instant travel. I can't quite decide.

Back at the apartment, I meet up with Gramps who's sitting out in the courtyard watching the neighbours come and go. I sit down beside him and tell him all about meeting Jesus in the hills, and I repeat everything he told me.

With a smile on his face, he says to me, 'I remember my personal meetings with the Lord. The first time was down by the canal and then another time it was in Fountain Square. We really value such precious moments with the Lord.'

I also share with Gramps my thoughts about how different things are in heaven in relation to time and eternity.

Gramps looks thoughtful and then says, 'I well remember when Grandma and I met you, shortly after you arrived in heaven. It seemed to us as though it was just yesterday, when we last saw you in our home in Newbury. It was the same when your Uncle Frank arrived. In heaven there's no awareness of time spent waiting to be reunited with loved ones and friends. And, as much as we were so happy to see you again, we never felt lonely or sad without you.'

I nod in agreement and tell Gramps, 'I look forward to meeting up with Uncle Frank sometime. He was such a help to me as a new Christian and taught me a lot about prayer.'

With a flash of inspiration in his face, Gramps suddenly says, 'Jamie, I've just had an idea. You should go to the Observatory in the city centre. There you can see for yourself what's happening across the earth. It's a remarkable place to visit. Each time your grandma and I have been there, we've seen many angels who came to watch too. They are so curious to see how God's plan is being outworked among the different nations.'

'Wow,' I respond, 'That does sound exciting. I think I'll go there now.'

'About time,' Gramps replies, with a twinkle in his eye.

THE OBSERVATORY

Finding the Observatory should be easy due to the fact I've spotted its tall, distinctive dome on previous visits to the city centre. On reaching Throne Square, I head in a westerly direction to take a short walk across to Asher Street. Unsurprisingly, the highway is busy with pedestrians, most of who seem to be making their way towards the city centre.

I get a great view along the golden highway with row after row of buildings on either side, as far as the eye can see. Asher Street's magnificent four storey buildings, with their ornate balconies, have been designed and built using the exquisite, clear-blue hyacinth gemstone.

It was Thaniel who first told me about the twelve gemstones, which were chosen by God as the perfect foundation for each of the city's entrances. I've also discovered something practical about heaven's colour scheme. The colours provide a helpful guide for new citizens, who are learning to find their way around the city. Each highway adopts a range of colours based on the primary gemstone. For example, the buildings on Asher Street use shades of lilac, blue, purple and violet.

While crossing a narrow lane, between two properties on the north side of the street, I catch a glimpse of the massive, white dome of the Observatory. Turning into the lane, it's just 100 metres before I reach the gardens surrounding the giant circular rotunda. Standing for a moment on the manicured lawn, I survey the building in front of me. The circular walls are built from blue Jade and are windowless, except for a series of narrow openings. These are positioned just below the lower edge of the dome, allowing easy access for the angels. The crystal dome rises to around fifty metres, and the outer diameter of the building is about 100 metres.

Behind me I hear a man's voice with a distinctive accent.

'Is this your first visit to the Observatory?' he asks.

I turn around to see a tall, slim man, who's aged about forty with short, brown hair, and wearing a white robe and gold crown. He looks at me with piercing, grey-blue eyes and a big, friendly smile.

'Hi there', I answer, adding, 'Yes, it's my first time and I've been told that it's a great place to visit, and one I wouldn't want to miss.'

I'm quietly wondering to myself about his shining crown. Although I see plenty of people wearing crowns, this is my first opportunity to meet someone actually wearing one. I hope to find out more later.

'My name's Pieter,' he continues. He then raises his arm and points toward the Observatory.

'Would you like me to show you the way inside?' he asks.

I now recognise his South African accent. It's very similar to a friend I used to know at university.

'Yes Pieter, that would be great. Oh and my name's Jamie,' I reply, and follow him.

Walking with Pieter, on the path that runs alongside the lawn, we follow the gentle curve of the clear-blue building, until we reach the main entrance. Passing a small group of young people waiting excitedly outside, we go in.

The entrance lobby is large and has a low ceiling and wide corridors that bend to the right and the left. There are hundreds of people moving about, and there's much animated conversation. I keep close to Pieter, as he confidently makes his way along the corridor to the right. We pass several entrances on our left, until he leads me through his chosen doorway, which brings us into the auditorium. Light streams in through the white, translucent dome, casting an ambient glow across the interior. We walk down the sloping aisle and sit down in one of the many rows of seats. There's a great feeling of anticipation. The spacious building is alive with the faint hum of people, who are all talking in hushed tones. With no real idea of what to expect, I'm excited and can't wait for what's about to happen. Questions race through my mind.

'How will I feel observing scenes on earth? Why does heaven watch such events across the nations? How helpful will this experience be?'

No one can miss the huge, white wall that curves round in front us. The smooth surface flows seamlessly up to the domed ceiling and covers a third of the circular auditorium to the right and left.

I briefly look up at the vast space inside the Observatory. Glancing behind me, I see there are three different levels of seating. This allows several thousand people to get a perfect view of the wide, curved wall, which forms the viewing screen. The building looks crammed with citizens, and among them are plenty of enthusiastic young people.

Overhead is the massive crystal dome, with its circular opening in the centre, known as an oculus. About a thousand angels are gathered together near the roof of the dome. Dressed in their white robes, their glowing faces are all turned toward the wall. The angels remain silent and appear as eager as everyone else to see what's about to be shown.

I turn to Pieter to put a question to him that I just have to ask. I hesitate, not quite sure how else to say it.

So in a whisper I ask slowly, 'Is this place a cinema?'

As soon as the words are out of my mouth I feel silly. A cinema in heaven! Did I really say that? What will he think of me?

Pieter replies with a giggle, and is clearly amused at my choice of words. 'You could say that, but it's much more than a cinema. The Observatory isn't a place for entertainment; it's more about education and greater awareness. There are no blockbuster movies! What the angels and citizens observe here are real-time events taking place across the earth. The angels have been watching events here since time began. They are greatly interested in everything God does on planet earth. Remember, the angels saw God's creation of the universe and the exact positioning of the stars. The records report that this caused them to all to shout for joy.'

Pieter is keen to explain more. 'In the Observatory, we watch young evangelists risking their lives to share the gospel. There are often scenes of men and women engaged in continuous prayer that changes nations. Sometimes we see great outpourings of God's power upon the church. There are examples of compassionate care given in the name of Messiah Jesus. At other times, we witness the people of God praising and worshiping. The angels speak of a future time in this Observatory when some will watch the judgement of God fall upon evil regimes, and on those who have systematically opposed the kingdom of God.'

The blast of a muted trumpet somewhere overhead, causes a sudden hush to fall across the Observatory. On the large white wall appears a view that's familiar to me. The scale of the image is massive, and the shapes and colours appear in high definition. It's an aerial image of Jerusalem, Israel. I recognise the golden roof of the Dome on the Rock as a flock of white doves rise above the ancient Western Wall, and circle above a towering minaret nearby. A few women wearing traditional black dresses and headscarves make their way purposefully across an open concourse. Men wearing skull caps and casual clothes enter and leave the different buildings.

Pieter speaks to me in soft tones, 'Heaven keeps a constant watch over Jerusalem and the land of Israel. The city of Jerusalem is at the heart of God's eternal plan. This is the land where Messiah Jesus is expected to appear for the second time. The rebirth of the nation of Israel in 1948 and the reunification of Jerusalem in 1967 were sovereign acts of Almighty God. We also read in the Revelation of St. John that this city of heaven will be relocated to the new earth, and will be known as the New Jerusalem for eternity. It's no small wonder that there's so much conflict in the Middle East region, between the forces of good and evil.'

The picture zooms away from Jerusalem and within seconds I'm looking at the land mass of Israel, Syria, North Africa and the Eastern Mediterranean, from high over the earth. The angle changes and the view races back towards Egypt and the Nile Delta. I can see the busy Port of Alexandra, Port Said and the sprawling city of Cairo. The scene focuses down towards the south-east of the city, until it reaches a series of caves built into a tall cliff.

The entrances to the caves are decorated with Coptic Christian designs. Hundreds of people are entering one particularly large cave marked out with a sign, which reads ST SIMON THE TANNER. We begin to hear the sound of joyful singing as we view inside the underground cavern. Many thousands of worshippers, dressed in casual clothes, fill the dark cave. From the well-lit stage, prayers are offered in Arabic by a grey-bearded Coptic priest, who's dressed in his traditional black cap and cloak. All the people stand and call out in prayer with raised hands, asking God to bring peace to their city and to their land. The Arabic word for peace 'Salaam, salaam' is repeated many times. Then a small choir on the stage present a song of praise, accompanied by a flute. I can feel the presence of God among the worshippers, just as I do here in heaven.

Pieter quietly tells me, 'These people, called the Zabbaleen, are known as Cairo's garbage collectors. They represent some of Egypt's poorest people who were forced to flee to the Mokattam hills during the 1970's, from Giza, south of Cairo. From very small beginnings, the church there was founded with just a few children and several adults. God has worked among these Christian people as a witness to the nation and the world. The people have extended the natural cave systems to create an underground auditorium, which can accommodate up to 20,000 worshippers. There's also a monastery and education centre. It's even become something of a tourist attraction.'

I feel privileged to observe this gathering of God's people on earth. My heart rejoices to see for myself the church proclaiming God's kingdom, in the midst of conflict. As the scene pans out, everyone in the Observatory rises to their feet and we all thank and praise God for his works on the earth. Somehow, I know these prayers from the church in the cave are reaching God's throne in heaven.

At that moment, I realise that what I've just seen must be what the angels on earth observe. I'm sure I've read in the Bible about the watching angels, those who receive instructions to keep their eyes over the church and the work of God on the earth.

The panorama in front of us changes, and the focus moves across North Africa and the Atlantic Ocean, towards South America. Passing the large country of Brazil, we get closer to land-locked Paraguay and Asunción, its capital city beside the river. It's just before dawn, and we can see a large statue on the top of a small hill situated just south of the city. About a dozen people stand praying, I can hear prayers in both English and Spanish as the intercessors look out across the city with their hands held high. I recognise some of the language, 'el presidente, el gobierno y la economía,' as they pray for their president, the government and the economy. As the first light of dawn appears, the group continue to ask God to bring justice to their nation. Then they all pray out loud together, as they seek unity among the churches. Finally the sun breaks on the horizon, and they join together in a song of thanksgiving before returning down the hill and back into the city.

Everyone in the Observatory again rises to their feet. They also thank God for his work in Paraguay and the Latin American nations. After sitting down, I feel a gentle pat on my forearm and look round to see a grey-haired lady beside me. Her face is radiant and her eyes shine bright.

Looking straight at me, she says with a clear and gentle voice, 'For many years Christians have regularly climbed that steep road up the hill called Cerro Lambaré to pray before dawn. It's part of a continuous ministry of prayer that God is raising up across Asunción, Paraguay's capital. Through persistent prayer the believers in Paraguay are seeing God transform their nation. I was a missionary in Paraguay for many years, and I've seen how the number of born-again believers has grown and the nation has prospered.'

'Thank you so much,' I say as I witness another moment of perfect timing.

I realise that these faithful Christians in Paraguay have no awareness that heaven is watching their service for God. How encouraging it would be for them to know the saints in heaven are rejoicing about their commitment to the gospel. Also for them to recognise that God sends his angels to protect his people and their work for him on earth.

It makes me think about something mentioned in a New Testament letter. The writer to the Hebrews reminds the Christians that they are *"surrounded by a great cloud of witnesses"*. Every citizen in heaven, including the men and women of faith under the old covenant, is given the privilege to become one of the many witnesses. We are like spectators in a grand stadium, who watch the progress of believers and cheer them on as they run their race.

As the scene before us returns to watch over the city of Jerusalem, Pieter turns to me and tells me more about his own life.

'I was busy serving God with my wife Sue and our three children. We lived in Cape Town and were on the leadership team of a large Pentecostal church. I'd been to Bible School in Johannesburg and had a teaching ministry as part of the church outreach programme. I loved travelling around South Africa and into neighbouring Rwanda. My whole life was given over to serving God.'

He continues, 'One day while out surfing at Scarborough Beach with a friend from church, I got caught in a powerful rip current and died as a result of drowning. The next thing I remember was walking towards the light and the gates of heaven.'

Pieter touches the crown on his head and says, 'I received this crown in the Hall of Honours, and only wear it because of my wife and children. I miss them all but feel so proud knowing they continue to serve God without me. I wear my crown for their sakes until they join me here.'

I'm deeply touched by Pieter's story, and to hear about his tragic accident while out surfing. I also had experienced the thrill of surfing, when I learned to ride the waves while on holiday with friends. But now, tears fill my eyes as I listen to Pieter and think about his wife and family in Cape Town. They must miss him so much. How glad they would be to know of his joy and service for God in heaven.

I struggle to respond, 'Thank you... Pieter, your testimony is very powerful. I really appreciate you approaching me outside the Observatory. It's really good to meet you.'

Pieter's story gets me thinking of my own family, my younger brother Josh, and two older sisters Suzie and Sarah who are both married. I also miss my sweet girlfriend, Catherine, who lives in Oxford. I hope she's not too sad. She will make someone a lovely wife.

Pieter says, 'God is good. I now know he's called me to serve him as a teacher in heaven's University, to prepare citizens to rule on the new earth.'

University? There's a university in heaven? Pieter's mention of his own involvement suddenly grabs my attention. Although I feel very blessed to hear about Pieter's family and service for God, I can't stop thinking about heaven's University. It all sounds very interesting, but it's hard to imagine which topics are taught. I think back to my six years spent studying architecture at the University of Bath, before joining the architectural practice in Abingdon.

I ask, 'Pieter, would you be able to show me around heaven's University? It all sounds so fascinating.'

'Of course I will. We can go afterwards.' He replies.

New images appear on the wall, and we see the coast of West Africa; the view begins to focus on north-eastern Nigeria. The landscape is mostly rural until the scene draws close to a large city with highways, parks and an airport to the east. The airport welcome sign reads Katsina Airport. In the nearby city, hundreds of believers are calling out to God in a large church building. Two Roman Catholic priests are praying over a row of five coffins, each draped with a plain white cloth. The coffins rest on stands placed side by side in front of the altar. Many people are visibly crying with grief over the loss of friends and loved ones.

Pieter quietly explains to me, 'It appears that the deaths of these Christians are the direct result of an atrocity. All across the northern states of Nigeria, believers are facing unprecedented attacks and persecution from religious terrorists. Some have fled to the south, where the majority of the population are Christians. But most remain in the Muslim-dominated north, trusting God for his protection as they witness about the Messiah Jesus. There's a constant threat of danger with regular kidnappings, shootings, bombings and church buildings being set on fire.'

On the screen we watch as a group of around twenty Nigerian women pray in front of the coffins. Wearing brightly coloured blouses and skirts with matching headpieces, they stretch out their hands. Tears roll down their cheeks, as they call on God, in their hour of need.

'Come Lord Jesus, Come soon Lord Jesus, Come quickly to redeem your people.' They cry out together.

High in the Observatory dome, I notice a sudden movement among the angels. A third of their number disappears from view, leaving through the dome's circular opening. I get the distinct impression that the angels have been signalled into action, in response to the prayers of the Nigerian women.

Pieter confirms this to me by explaining in a hushed tone, 'The cry of the martyrs has been heard. Angels have immediately been sent to strengthen the church in Nigeria. The angels know exactly what to do, because they've been commissioned at their headquarters. They provide instant, unseen aid and comfort. Believers on earth rarely see the angels with their own eyes. Though sometimes a prophetic vision of angelic activity is given to a faithful witness.'

Pieter knows so much about heaven and it's really good for me to learn from him. I'm so glad he offered to bring me in here.

The scene on the white wall changes. The same group of Nigerian women begin to sing with their rich, deep voices. They start to swing their arms and sway their bodies from side to side; dancing with delight in front of the congregation. It's as though they understand the joys of heaven that await those whose lives on earth have ended so brutally.

This makes me think about these latest martyrs who have been killed for the sake of the Gospel. Even before their bodies were placed in funeral coffins, their souls have already arrived in heaven. Dressed in pure white robes they will have walked towards the entrance gates full of expectation. I feel so sure they received a rapturous welcome. I know something of their joy when they meet God face to face, and begin to experience their wonderful church family here in heaven. Maybe I will get to meet them!

'Pieter, the Observatory is an incredible place. I feel so privileged to witness the events taking place on earth. It gives me a fresh perspective on the way situations are viewed from heaven. I see the greatness of God's love as he reaches out from heaven to a world that is lost, confused and sometimes deceived. His gift of salvation remains available to all. The witness of the church to the nations clearly remains God's top priority.'

Pieter smiles and replies, 'Yes, I agree with you. I'm confident that God will fulfil his plan of salvation. But there will also be justice for the martyrs, and judgement against all those who oppose the rule of God.'

The scene on the white wall changes again. Crossing Africa and the Indian Ocean the focus turns toward rural south-west China. A group of around 200 people, mostly women, have gathered at the riverside for Christian baptism. Dressed in casual clothes and in bare feet they line up to give their testimonies, before being invited into the river. Standing in the water are two grey-haired Chinese pastors, who receive each new believer in turn. After each new believer declares Jesus as Lord and Saviour, they cross their arms and are swiftly plunged backwards under the muddy waters.

Emerging with great joy on their faces and some with arms raised high, they wade back to the bank of the river. They are greeted by their close friends, who offer white towels to wrap around themselves. The baptisms are unhurried and the waiting line gradually becomes shorter. Finally, the last new believer steps forward. He's a young man in his early teens. He shouts aloud his testimony and runs into the water to be baptised. He re-appears with a big wide smile on his face, and returning through the shallow water he runs out splashing with arms waving and shouting praises to God.

Following this scene, a huge roar of non-stop praise echoes around the Observatory. This must be the loudest sound I've heard in heaven. I'm sure it can be heard across the entire city centre. It's even louder than the reception at the city gates. I look up at the angels joining everyone else with spontaneous shouts of, 'Hallelujah', 'Thank you Jesus' and 'Praise the Lord'. It reminds me of the parable about the joy of the women and her friends, after she found the coin, which had been lost. Jesus taught the people, *'In the same way there is rejoicing in the presence of the angels of God over one sinner who repents.'*

Now I'm experiencing that special kind of rejoicing. Peiter can't stop laughing. He tries to say something to me, except it's in Afrikaans. He looks briefly at me and simply bursts into another fit of hysterics. A few moments ago he was caught up in praising God and now he's overflowing with joy and nothing can stifle it. All over the Observatory there are scores of people continuing to shout God's praises. A few are even jumping up and down with arms waving. Others are punching the air with gestures of victory. I've never experienced anything like this before; the whole atmosphere is infectious. I can only describe this as absolute joy in the presence of the Lord.

I decide to sit down like others are doing. Of course, Peiter is doubled up in laughter while standing, so he can't sit down! Gradually peace returns to the whole theatre and the outrageous joy and laughter is reduced to an occasional half-stifled chuckle. Many heads are bowed as the awareness of God's holy presence again fills the room. Pieter also finally slumps down beside me and remains motionless, with his eyes closed.

My visit to the Observatory has been a wonderful experience. Any questions I had have been answered. Viewing events taking place in earth-time displays the evidence of God's kingdom from an eternal perspective. I'm left realising that heaven is no glorified bubble. Heaven is God's supreme dwelling place and the eternal command centre of his kingdom. From heaven, God's rule extends to the ends of his creation, the earth, the universe, across all spiritual realms and invisible dimensions.

I look around and the auditorium is already half empty as people leave. Thankfully, Pieter is finally making sense.

'Jamie, I think it's time to leave.' he says.

'Okay, let's go,' I reply as I stand up to leave. Pieter lifts himself up cautiously; I think he still feels God's power all over him. We make our way back up the aisle, and follow the corridor back to the lobby.

As we walk along the garden path, Pieter asks, 'Jamie, am I taking you to the University?'

'That's what we agreed,' I respond, trying to hide my smile.

Pieter says, 'Well first, I need to collect my scrolls from the Library.'

'That's fine,' I say.

We walk back along Asher Street and cross Throne Square, discussing all we have just seen taking place on earth. It doesn't take long to reach the square in front of the Library. I tell Pieter that I'll wait while he picks up his manuscripts.

UNIVERSITY

Does everyone receive a perfect understanding of God and eternity the moment they arrive in heaven? Is our knowledge instantly complete and lacking nothing? I could almost have accepted this; however, I already know this isn't what happened to me. For a start, only God knows absolutely everything. Omniscience is a divine attribute that's reserved for God alone. The angels too have only limited information and they've lived here since the time of creation. Thaniel, my guardian angel is very knowledgeable. That's why he's been assigned to help me learn about the heavenly life. However, he doesn't know everything, and he remains very curious about many aspects of God's purposes and plans. He has little understanding about the future. He's no idea when Jesus Messiah will establish his kingdom on the earth, with the New Jerusalem at its centre.

For me, the reality is this. Since arriving in heaven, I've been learning more about this great city from those around me. This happens naturally, as I spend time with my friends, catch up with my grandparents and listen to what the angels say.

I'm so glad not to be stuck for ever with the limited knowledge I gained on earth in almost thirty years. The thought of never being able to develop my understanding or expand my abilities is now unimaginable.

Heaven offers me unlimited opportunities to grow in wisdom and to increase my intellectual capacity. This is true for everyone, from the youngest child to the oldest person. This is a place where even infants can speak with infinite wisdom. Gone are the barriers for learning found on earth, whether from disability, emotional trauma or simply growing older. Here in the city, everyone shares a quest to fully know God and has an enthusiasm for learning more about his ways.

Everywhere I go I make fresh discoveries; there are so many new places to explore and things to experience. The most transforming catalyst is

God's presence, which reaches out with love and immense power. After meeting God face to face in the Throne Room, I began to change the way I think about everything, including events in my past life. The city is a truly inspirational place for me to advance my knowledge and learn from those around me. I appreciate the fact that nothing is forced, and there's also a welcome absence of self-opinionated people!

Pieter, who I first met at the Observatory, has agreed to take me to the University where he teaches. He's gone into the Library to collect some manuscripts. Meanwhile, I'm sat on one of the many carved benches in Library Square waiting for him to emerge. It's not long before he's walking straight towards me, with a clutch of scrolls under his arm.

'There you are Jamie, I said I wouldn't be long,' he announces, with a big smile.

'I've been fine,' I reply. 'There's plenty to think about.'

We set off together and soon reach the honey-gold buildings of Zebulun Street, before crossing the canal bridge and turning into Miriam Avenue.

 I ask, 'Well Pieter, what are you talking about in your next lecture?'

He answers, 'I'll be talking about the unity of the church. The apostle Paul will be the main speaker this time; I'm so looking forward to it. We'll be explaining more about the advice written by Paul himself. As you know, Paul wrote an important letter to the church in Ephesus, and he has much to say on the topic of unity.'

'The apostle Paul?' I say to myself. This is going to be very special.

'Can I come along to listen?' I ask, feeling a little uncertain about the arrangements.

'Yes, of course,' Pieter responds. 'All the lectures, tutorials and facilities are freely open to every citizen. You'll see what's on by reading the notices at the main entrance.'

Walking along the avenue, I glance down at the beautiful, sparkling water of the canal. It looks as clear and refreshing as ever. I'm suddenly aware that I'm really thirsty to learn more about God's ways. We soon arrive at the University campus, located on Gad Street, south west of the city centre.

I'm always fascinated when I see new buildings, mainly because of my architectural training. I get my first good look at the University. The campus includes a group of similar buildings, which are linked together and standing around twenty metres tall. Constructed from a delightful, apple-green crystal, the four storey structures have rows of windows with small balconies, which face out across the city.

We approach the large, arched entrance of the nearest building, and walk under the broad headstone with the inscription, UNIVERSITY. I spot the notices on the inner wall and walk over with Pieter right behind me. We join a group of people who are carefully reading all the information. It's neatly written on sheets of parchment, which are pasted along the archway. Quickly, I scan the range of subjects; Arts and Music, Church Life, Creation and Science, History and Purpose, Kingdom Government, Divine Law, New Heaven and New Earth, Spiritual Warfare, Theology.

I turn to Pieter, 'They all sound fascinating. Which topics do you teach?'

He replies, 'Church Life and Theology mostly. The teaching staff includes; apostles, missionaries, evangelists, reformers, along with many well-known church leaders and theologians. Mind you, some of the theologians freely admit they've changed their views quite radically, since arriving in heaven!' That makes me smile.

As we enter the campus I find myself walking through a spacious, courtyard cloister in the shape of a pentagon. It's surrounded by five large square buildings, perfectly angled and each one around seventy metres wide. They are connected on both the ground level and first floor by a series of Roman-style arched porticos, which are supported by tall

Ionic columns. Many citizens are walking under the pale-green porticos, as they move between the different buildings. In the centre of the courtyard is a large, circular garden with an abundance of flowering shrubs and ground-cover plants. Pieter stops by the fountain in the centre of the garden.

Suddenly, I recognise Ishran, as he arrives through one of the entrances. It's great to see him and he's heading our way.

As he gets nearer, I call out, 'Ishran'.

He sees me at once and walks quickly towards us.

He says, 'Jamie, it's good to see you.'

I waste no time and do the introductions, 'Ishran, this is Pieter, and he's a lecturer and a friend of mine.'

Pieter looks carefully at Ishran and says, 'Hi Ishran, I think I've seen you in my lectures.'

'Yes, you have,' says Ishran, 'I'm doing the Church Life course.'

I tell Ishran, 'Well, that's where I'm going too - except it's my first time.'

'We had better be going,' says Pieter, as we all head towards the building on our right.

While walking across the cloister, I tell Ishran about my recent visit to the Observatory and how I met Pieter. I explain to him about the astonishing things we saw on earth, the different gatherings of Christians in Egypt, Paraguay and Nigeria, along with the baptisms in China.

We enter the doorway and climb up the steps that lead to the lecture hall. Pieter turns and waves his hand.

He says, 'You go through and I'll see you guys later.'

Still holding his tied scrolls, he disappears through a small door and into a side room. We enter the large lecture theatre, which holds about a 1,000 citizens, and is already two-thirds full. The clear, crystal ceiling slopes down towards the front where an emerald-green lecture table is positioned. Just behind the table are three high-backed seats. Looking around, there's a good mix of ages in the audience. I'm really excited about what I will learn.

Through a small, arched side-entrance at the front enter three people. The first lecturer is an elderly man, with bright eyes and an olive complexion, who I imagine to be from the Mediterranean. A smaller man follows, and he looks distinctively Chinese. He has a round, smiling face and grey hair swept across one side his head. Then my friend Pieter follows on behind; he's still wearing his crown.

Everyone stands, and the room goes quiet. The first lecturer raises both hands and thanks God for his faithfulness, for his promises and for his purposes in heaven and on earth.

'Amen, amen,' everyone responds. Then we all quickly sit down.

'Let me introduce the speakers for this session,' says the lecturer. 'As many of you will know, I'm Paul, apostle to many nations. Next to me is my dear friend, Watchman Nee, apostle to China and once again we have, Pieter Vorster, apostle to South Africa.'

There's loud cheering and hand clapping for several moments, until Paul raises his hand to start. I can hardly believe what I'm seeing. To think, the apostle Paul himself is standing in front of us and ready to share more of the truth about God and his church. I'm awestruck. If that wasn't enough I've also read many of the writings of the second lecturer, Watchman Nee. His books on the Christian life and the local church were very influential, especially during my early years as a Christian. What a privilege to hear Watchman speak. I know he has a deep grasp of the truth of the Bible. Then my friend Pieter - I get the feeling he rather understated his ministry in South Africa.

Paul says, 'Firstly, let's hear from Watchman.'

Watchmen Nee steps forward to address us. In a soft, clear voice, Watchman begins his talk. 'Early in my Christian life, God opened my eyes to the great need for local churches to be raised up among every community. It was his will, from the beginning, to establish witnesses among each neighbourhood and family. There is one church, only one true church. She is the body and chosen bride of Messiah Jesus. There is one church, here in heaven, without any division on the basis of either doctrine or styles of worship. We are joined together by the love of God and the sacrifice of Messiah on the cross. The single point of difference between us is our varied service for God. This arises from his eternal call on our lives. The church on earth is not a different body. She is joined to us and part of us. She will be a pure church, a spotless church and a united church.'

He continues, 'The testimony of unity is the greatest witness to the risen Lord. There are different gifts, various ministries, but one body whether on earth or here in heaven. Each saint lives, not for themselves, but for others. The church shall forever be a glorious church, filled with God's glory. God wants not merely individual pursuit of victory or spirituality but a corporate, glorious church presented to himself here in heaven.'

Watchman Nee gently bows his head toward the audience, and sits down behind the desk. No one moves and there's a profound silence in the lecture hall.

Then the apostle Paul stands up to speak. Every eye is fixed on him.

'My fellow saints, it was for this purpose that Christ died, was buried, and was raised up. He returned to his throne of glory at God's right hand, in order to establish his church; the community of people chosen from every nation. This church is the body of Christ on the earth, as well as in heaven, and each member must recognise their own gifts and calling from God. Our aim is to serve one another in love.'

'We are the witnesses of Jesus in heaven as we were on earth. For whether on earth or in heaven we are one with the Lord. Some valued their lives on earth more than in the promised heaven. I wish it were not so. To be with the Lord, whether on earth or in heaven, should be the aim of every citizen. Our service for God on earth reaps its rewards in heaven. Here, we continue to serve and fulfil God's eternal purpose in Christ - a kingdom, which lasts forever. Amen.' Paul lowers his head, and returns to his seat.

Finally, Pieter stands and moves forward to speak. 'My friends, my brothers and sisters in God's family, I encourage you. The truth is that we serve God alongside our loved ones who believe on earth. We serve in the fullness of revelation and in full view of the city of God. Those on earth serve with partial understanding and long to even glimpse this place. Their service, through the church, is by faith and with hope in their hearts. Our service, as part of the same body of Messiah, is by sight. Seeing all things in heaven, with our very own eyes, we are filled with the glory of God. We stand alongside those who battle for righteousness on the earth. We watch the angels of God bring strength to the weary and aid for the suffering. Until the time arrives, when the whole church shall be gathered together in this place, we wait for them to join us. Then, we shall all stand together to sing the Song of the Lamb, before the throne of God.'

Pieter bows his head for a moment and steps back; the three speakers then leave the room. Everyone remains quietly in their seats as they fully absorb the teaching and concepts, which have just been shared.

One of the great benefits of life in heaven is the ability to remember things. Everyone, children and adults alike, has perfect memory of everything they experience in heaven. The things we now hear and sights we see are never forgotten, and can be recalled anytime in minute detail. There's no need to take notes, set ourselves reminders or keep journals. Everything is retained. I marvel at this new-found capacity to hold on to knowledge and truth forever.

Eventually, Ishran stands up to leave and says, 'I'm off to the next lecture, Jamie. Are you coming?' I know from the tone of his voice that he expects me to agree.

'Sounds good. Who will be speaking next time?' I ask, as I quickly follow Ishran out of the lecture theatre.

He continues, 'It's the apostle John. He's speaking in the main lecture theatre. It's a brilliant talk about the New Jerusalem, which he gives regularly. I do want to hear it again.'

We make our way under the portico into the next building and follow a line of people who are entering the main auditorium. There must be 2,000 people crowded into the spacious room. We manage to get a couple of seats, just two rows from the front, to the right of a large podium. The light streaming in through the crystal ceiling causes the polished, apple-green crystal walls to glow. I feel really motivated about listening to another great apostle of the church. The atmosphere is hushed and expectant.

A distinguished-looking man enters the room.

Around me I hear several whispers of, 'It's John.'

Wearing a purple sash around his white robe, the apostle John carries a single scroll. On his head rests a golden crown. He briefly looks around the audience, his hair is white and his eyes are bright and intense. He moves with ease, and his whole posture is relaxed and reassuring. The elderly apostle takes his place at the podium and lays down his scroll. The tied cord around the scroll is quickly loosened. Carefully unrolling the scroll with his left hand, John holds the central rod in the other hand.

Finding the selected passage he begins to read, slowly and deliberately. A holy silence fills the room.

'And he carried me away in the Spirit to a great and high mountain, and showed me the holy city, Jerusalem, coming down out of heaven from God, having the glory of God.'

I immediately recognise the apostle's own words recorded in the Book of Revelation.

He continues, *'Her brilliance was like a very costly stone, as a stone of shining, crystal jasper. It had a great and high wall, with twelve gates, and at the gates twelve angels; and names were written on them, which are the names of the twelve tribes of the sons of Israel. There were three gates on the East, and three gates on the North, and three gates on the South, and three gates on the West. And the wall of the city had twelve foundation stones, and on them were the twelve names of the twelve apostles of the Lamb.'*

John pauses for a few moments and everyone waits.

'This remains my testimony,' he declares with quiet authority, 'concerning eternal things, which I was able to see with my own eyes. I was brought to this place by the Spirit of the Lord. With one of the seven archangels as my guide, I set out on my first journey in heaven. Clearer, than any mortal man before me, I saw the glorious sights of the crystal city, designed and established by God himself. God chose me to be his witness and to publish the vision in my final book.'

The arrival of someone standing at the little door near to the podium creates a moment of distraction, which gets John's attention along with most of the audience. John smiles and waves to his waiting guest.

He says, 'Beatus, my good friend, come and join me here.'

A small elderly man, dressed in a simple, white linen robe, and carrying a single roll of parchment, steps forward and stands alongside the apostle.

John takes a good look at his guest, and then introduces him. 'I would like you all to meet my dear friend, Beatus of Liébana, in Spain.'

Ishran and I join the audience to politely clap our hands as a welcome.

John continues, 'Beatus is one of a select few, who saw for himself the reality of heaven, and presented it to his own generation. Almost 700 years after me, Beatus lived in a remote monastery, near Santander in northern Spain. He followed the steps of my recorded journey and spent long hours contemplating the great city with its twelve gates. As a man of much prayer and devotion, he worshipped the God of heaven and earth. Eventually, he felt compelled to write his own illustrated commentary, which was based on everything I had said concerning the end of the age. He used his skill as a communicator to portray the coming glory and judgement of God. Taking the words of my written revelation, which had been inspired by God himself, he used colour and image to paint the scenes of things to come.'

Turning to his friend, John says, 'Beatus, show us the record of your work, which you've brought from the Library?'

Beatus unrolls his parchment, and carefully holds the top and bottom of the curled manuscript to reveal the brightly coloured painting. From where I'm sitting, I can clearly see a plan of the New Jerusalem, a city laid out in a square grid, with bold patterns of red, orange, blue and gold. There are three gates on each of the four sides of the city, and a different robed figure stands in each of the twelve arched entrances. At the centre of the painting is the image of the Lamb, Jesus Messiah. Alongside the Lamb, stands an angel with a golden measuring rod, and there's also someone holding a book, who appears to be the apostle John himself.

John looks closely at the illuminated page, as if he's seen it many times before.

Pointing with his hand, John says, 'Here we see the names of the twelve apostles assigned to their gates. Above each apostle is a gemstone, identified by its own name. These are the same precious stones used in the foundations of each gate. In this visual illustration, the focus is on the church and her apostles, there is no mention of the tribes of Israel.'

Beatus continues to hold up his picture to give everyone a clear view of the image. He slowly turns toward the audience on his right, then turns to the left, and afterwards returns to the centre.

John asks us, 'Are you able to understand something more about the design and plan of heaven?'

At that moment I remember the powerful words of Jesus spoken to me on the hillside.

John continues and his voice grows stronger. 'The city is built on the foundation of the apostles of the church, yet at the same time heaven honours the accomplishment of each of the twelve sons of Jacob. In his illuminated manuscript, Beatus positioned each gemstone in precisely the same order that I had recorded on my journey around the city.'

Turning back to his own scroll, John slowly reads out aloud, *'The first foundation was Jasper, the second Sapphire, the third Chalcedony, the fourth Emerald, the fifth Onyx, the sixth Sardius, the seventh Chrysolite, the eighth Beryl, the ninth Topaz, the tenth Chrysoprase, the eleventh Jacinth, and the twelfth Amethyst.'*

John then points toward Beatus, who's still holding up his picture, and says, 'Written in Latin, are the names of the apostles and gemstones shown in consecutive order, starting with the gate on the top left corner of the city. The list begins with Peter at the gate with the jasper foundation. Each of the other apostles is then named consecutively around the square of the city. You can see for yourselves that the list continues in a clockwise direction, which ends with Matthew at the gate with the amethyst foundation.'

'Some have found mystery in the ordering of the apostles shown in the manuscript of Beatus, but the matter can easily be resolved. As many of you already know, Greek and Latin script, as well as English writing, always starts from the left and is read across to the right. However, in Hebrew and other Semitic languages the opposite is true. All words are written and read starting from the right side.'

'For example, the prophet Ezekiel in his own vision of the holy city lists each series of gates in the order he saw them; that is from right to left. Ezekiel names the three gates on the East side of the city wall, and lists them as follows; Joseph, Benjamin and Dan. However, written down in the original Hebrew text, the sequence of these gates would appear to readers as Dan - Benjamin - Joseph. In the same way, the direction of the northern gates would be seen as Levi - Judah - Reuben.'

Beatus nods his clear agreement while John makes his point.

Turning to his friend he asks, 'Beatus, do you have anything to say here?'

Beatus lays down his manuscript and facing the audience replies, 'Yes, I used the Latin rule, writing from left to right, as understood at that time by the church and the wider society. My listing of the first six apostles was effectively a mirror image of the Hebrew listing and therefore appears in reverse order.'

'The order in which each tribe of Israel was assigned to the twelve gates was already established by Ezekiel. So I followed your list of gemstones, starting from the East, exactly as you had recorded. It was in my heart to honour the names of the apostles, the names you saw but did not record. These names had been passed down in this order by the early

126

church fathers. It was my wish to thank God for each of the apostles and to set each one at his own gate. '

'Precisely,' John replies to Beatus, Your work was never aligned to the modern compass point of North, but rather to the Orient. Since the beginning of time, all orientation started from the East; the direction of the rising sun. Now let me explain my journey in heaven in more detail.'

John pauses, as if to choose his words with great care. I'm so fascinated by the lecture and wonder what the apostle will say next.

'During my exile on the Isle of Patmos, before the Lord called me home, I received a series of visions from God, and all my reports were recorded in the Book of Revelation. I was invited by an archangel to enter a doorway to heaven, which led to my journey around the city. The archangel brought me first to the East wall of the city.'

'Above the first of the pearl gates I saw the inscription JOSEPH GATE. I knew the Joseph Gate was the first gate on the Orient wall, because of the ancient prophecy of Ezekiel. But I was truly amazed to also discover the name of PETER, APOSTLE, cut into the gate's red jasper foundation. My dear friend, Peter from Galilee, who was the first to believe that Jesus of Nazareth was the Messiah. He was also the first apostle of the church to be appointed by Jesus. His very name 'Petros' signified the rock upon which the new church was to be built.'

John continues, 'The angelic guide used a golden rod to carefully measure out the length and height of the walls and the gates. I was instructed to write down the measurements and descriptions of the gemstones. We then turned to our right, and walked beside the wall in a northerly direction.'

'After a great distance we passed the second entrance, the BENJAMIN GATE and later on, the DAN GATE before the wall turned square to the left. Three more gates awaited us along the northern edge of the holy city. From right to left they were the RUEBEN GATE, the JUDAH GATE and then the LEVI GATE.'

'We reached the entrance to the Levi Gate, which was built on a ruby-red foundation made of sardius and dedicated to the priests of Israel. So far, each series of three gates along the East and North had followed the exact listing of tribes, as recorded by the prophet Ezekiel in the Hebrew Scriptures.'

'I also observed each of the names of my fellow apostles that had been carved into the shining crystal foundations for each gate. Etched into the deep red foundation of the Levi Gate was the name of JAMES, APOSTLE. He was my very own brother, who was killed with sword, as a faithful martyr. I stood for a long time at the gate and wept. I knew James was here in the city, along with Peter and most of the other apostles, spending eternity with the Lord they loved.'

I'm totally gripped by this account, as John recalls his own personal journey in heaven. He's still so passionate about the vision that was given to him. There's no thought about Ishran beside me, or anyone else, as I wait for the apostle to continue. I feel sure that John has more to say.

Looking up at his attentive audience, John makes a direct appeal.

'My beloved friends, I want you to remember the unexpected direction I took, as I followed the archangel around the city. From my written summary of this journey, you will observe that I went from the East to the North, and then from the South to the West. So let me ask you this question? How was it possible to pass directly from the North to the South?'

Everyone waits in total silence hoping that the apostle will answer.

John resumes his explanation. 'At the Levi Gate, with its blood-red crystal foundation, the measurements were taken and I completed my notes. I prepared to walk on further with the archangel, following the anti-clockwise direction in which we were travelling. But to my astonishment, the archangel did not turn to climb back down the steps. Instead, he entered the gate into the city. I followed closely behind without questioning.

Unaware of our presence, crowds of people were also entering the city and there was much joy. We walked along the golden highway between the packed and noisy grandstands. The city was filled with citizens and angels. We quickly made our way along Levi Street and soon reached the tall buildings of the city centre. At first I was puzzled because there was no great temple to be found. Seeing the perplexed look on my face, the archangel said to me "The Lord God Almighty and The Lamb is the temple" and immediately I understood and felt at peace.'

'I went inside God's Throne Room and spent much time in worship before Messiah, who is the Lamb and the one I love. I also saw the cherubim and seraphim. My angelic guide invited me to stand in front of God's rainbow throne. For a short while, I stood beside the elders, but could not see their faces because the glory cloud was thick around the throne. I heard the saints of God sing with the angels to declare God's praises. The archangel also showed me where the stream flowed from under the throne and out into the street. All these things I recorded in my book.

I longed to see my brother James as I searched among the faces of the citizens; but our reunion was clearly being kept for a future occasion. The archangel and I continued to make our way through the vast city along the same diagonal direction from the northwest, until we reached a gate at the south eastern corner. As I passed through the arch in the wall and looked back above the entrance, I read the inscription, SIMEON GATE.'

'Then, as I looked down at the name etched into the honey-gold chrysolite foundation, I was totally unprepared for what I saw. It was my very own name; it read simply JOHN, APOSTLE. Tears again filled my eyes as I remembered my Lord Messiah's promise. He said he would go and prepare a place for all those who believed in him. I knew I would return to this city for ever, perhaps it would be soon.'

John continues, 'Turning right as I exited at the gate, the archangel continued to measure the length of the southern wall. We passed the ISSACHAR GATE followed by the ZEBULUN GATE. At the next corner we turned right again to follow the great wall along the western side of the city with the GAD GATE, the ASHER GATE and finally the NAPHTALI GATE. It was at the twelfth gate where the name of my dear friend and fellow apostle, MATTHEW was written into the lovely amethyst foundation.'

'So this was the way I saw all twelve gates, with three on each side of our magnificent foursquare city. It is truly remarkable that the names of each of the twelve sons of Jacob, along with all twelve apostles were known and recorded by God in heaven before creation.'

I'm fascinated by the explanation of the journey taken by the apostle John through the city and his explanation of the East, North, South and West route.

Unexpectedly, John asks his audience, 'Does anyone have a question at this point?'

He then points towards the back of the lecture theatre and asks, 'Do you have a question?'

Almost everyone on the front rows turns around to see a young man standing up to ask John a question. He's about my own age and has short, fair hair.

He asks, 'I would like to know if you think that Jesus Messiah, our great High Priest, entered the city by way of the Levi Gate with its crimson foundation?'

John replies, 'An interesting question, young man, is this your understanding?'

He answers, 'Yes, I believe I it is.'

'Well, I agree with you,' John responds confidently with a broad smile.

John's reply causes many to chuckle to themselves, as the inquisitive young man sits down and looks pleased. As for me, I now appreciate that heaven was never intended to be a showpiece, to be simply admired from the outside. It's a city with open gates that we can enter, a place to be enjoyed, and a realm filled with the presence of Almighty God.

John begins to sum up his talk. 'We see that Beatus identifies the name of the apostle inscribed into the foundation of each gate. Here is the list in its order. In the East, we begin with Peter, then Andrew and Judas, who was the son of James. They are followed along the north by Simon the Zealot, Bartholomew and my own brother, James. Then along the southern side, from East to West, we find my name, John, and then Philip followed by Judas. Yes, this was my close friend Judas Iscariot who was chosen to be among the Twelve, but destined to betray the Messiah.'

Along the front row, one of the younger citizens shoots up her hand to ask a question.

John smiles and asks, 'Do you also have a question?'

The young woman stands to speak.

'I do,' she replies and then looking directly at the apostle, she asks, 'My question is this. Did Judas Iscariot enter heaven?'

Several citizens in the audience gasp at the mention of Judas Iscariot, and the atmosphere is on a knife-edge as the young woman sits down to await John's reply.

John answers her, 'This is a good question and one I've been asked many times. Thank you for raising it again. The truth is that I have not seen Judas in heaven, I know of no-one who has seen him, and he is certainly not among the honourable men who stand before the throne of God.'

John pauses and then adds, 'Remember, that after the tragic death of Judas, Matthias was chosen to take his place among the twelve apostles, and he is here. All we know is that Judas awaits the Judgement Day, along with all who turn their back on God and reject his offer of salvation.'

The young woman who asked the question nods her appreciation and says, 'Thank you, John.'

Unfazed by the question, John resumes his talk, 'Now how far did we get along the city wall? Ah, yes, the western wall. The final three inscriptions in the foundations of the gates are James, the son of Alpheus, Thomas and Matthew.'

John then turns to Beatus and says, 'Thank you for your work that brought attention to the revelation of heaven's city. This is the New Jerusalem, the promised bride of Messiah Jesus; she is greatly loved and adorned with her crown.'

John steps back from the podium and there follows spontaneous cheering and clapping, which breaks out across the audience with Ishran and I joining in. John raises his hand in farewell and quietness returns to the lecture theatre. After rolling up and tying his scroll, he leaves the room, and Beatus holding his roll of parchment, follows close behind.

Turning to Ishran I say, 'What a fantastic opportunity to learn from the lecturers who give these talks. It's a wonderful privilege for them to be able to serve God here in this way for all eternity.'

Ishran replies, 'I agree and that's why I just love attending the lectures here at the University. The teaching brings a fuller understanding of God and his kingdom. It demonstrates the great wisdom of God who always completes his plans and fulfils his purposes in people's lives.'

We join the many people who are leaving the lecture theatre and make our way out into the University's garden.

I ask, 'Ishran, do you think God wants each of us to serve him in heaven?'

Ishran answers, 'I'm sure he does. Serving God is the source of greatest joy. I can't ever imagine not serving him.'

'Well, I really want to understand more of God's plan and purpose, so that I can serve him too,' I respond.

'Jamie, you're a real friend to me. We've already had some great times together and I guess there are lots more in the future. I'm sure that God has something special for you to do.' Ishran adds.

Leaving the University, we make our way back to the city centre. I tell Ishran about my meeting with Jesus and the things he spoke into my life.

HALL OF HONOURS

Arriving back at my apartment, I discover an unopened letter addressed to me lying on the lounge table. Full of curiosity, I break open the small, clay seal and unroll the parchment to discover its contents. The style of handwriting reminds me of the beautiful calligraphy produced by the angels in the Library. It's a special invitation from the Lord inviting me to attend the crowning ceremony at the Hall of Honours. I've heard a lot about this special place and I'm immediately overjoyed about the prospect of going. To receive a crown from the Lord will be such a great honour and a special occasion. I hope to get a chance to hear the stories of other people too.

The letter also brings huge relief. I know from talking to my friend Pieter, that not every citizen receives an invitation to attend the crowning ceremony. He told me there's another ceremony to which invitations are sent. It's called the hearing and this also takes place at the Hall of Honours. But the hearing is for citizens whose service for God has not been judged worthy of special merit. Pieter told me that some believers fail to faithfully represent the kingdom of heaven, during their earthly lives. They compromise the honour of Jesus Messiah and place greater value on earthly things, rather than heavenly things. Although by God's grace, they secure eternal life and a place in heaven, they don't share the same honour as others. They are given no crown to wear. They have forfeited their right to some of the rewards provided to citizens in the heavenly city.

But, far worse are the unimaginable horrors of those who die without accepting Jesus as the Messiah. The torment of all who resist the offer of forgiveness and turn their backs on God and his laws must be hell.

It's an awesome prospect to know an account of your own life must be given. As I consider the crowning ceremony, I quickly think back over my life as a Christian. The times I prayed and read my Bible. The countless meetings I attended at church to worship God and share fellowship with other believers. During my time at college and later in my job there were many opportunities I took to live out my Christian life. I think of the money I gave to support the work of the church and its outreach missions. There were occasions when I confidently talked about my faith and other times when I could have spoken out more.

The Hall of Honours is located on Joseph Street, and situated halfway between Rachel Avenue and Miriam Avenue. I set off at once and on reaching Issachar Street, I make my way along the highway as far as Rachel Avenue. From there I follow the canal, in the direction of the south east part of the city centre. I keep thinking about the ceremony and what to expect.

'Jamie, Jamie, wait for me,' I hear a young woman's voice behind me.

I turn around and see Hannah running to catch up. It's been a while since I last saw her and talked together at the village square, while I was out for a walk in the hills. We hug each other.

'Hannah, how nice to see you again, how are you?' I ask.

'Well actually, I'm doing really well and have made lots of new friends since we last met. I now play the flute regularly in Praise Pavilion, and I just love it.' She answers with obvious enthusiasm.

I reply, 'That's so good to hear.' I then ask, 'Where are you off to now?'

'Well, I've received an invitation to the crowning ceremony at the Hall of Honours, and I'm on my way there.' Hannah answers.

'That's where I'm going too, look here's my invitation!' I say, as I take out the rolled-up letter from inside the front of my robe.

In no time at all we reach Joseph Street. It's a very smart looking street with large properties built using the exquisite, red jasper gemstone.

Lots of other people are out and about and walking the same way as us, with some stopping to greet their friends. The sound of singing can be heard not far away. This prompts Hannah to share more about her experiences in the pavilion. She tells me about some of the new dancers, who now take part in the performances. One of her new friends is called Karen.

I interrupt, 'Not Karen, my niece who is one of the youth dancers?'

'What a coincidence,' Hannah replies, 'She told me she's the only Karen in the dance group. Isn't that just the kind of thing you expect in heaven?' she adds with a smile.

I'm so pleased about their friendship.

Hannah continues, 'At the pavilion, there's a brand new song and dance routine, praising God as Creator, it was written and performed by the children themselves.'

'That must be the performance I saw, even the angels joined in,' I reply.

'Yes, they do. It takes everyone by surprise,' she adds.

Hannah appears really happy to be playing flute in the orchestra on a regular basis. This reminds me about what Jediah, her guardian angel, had said about serving God in heaven.

After crossing the canal, we walk on down Joseph Street and I'm keen to tell Hannah about my recent discovery.

'Hannah, have you been to the University yet?' I ask.

'No, not yet, but a couple of my friends in the orchestra have said how inspirational it is. They've been a few times. I think I'll go soon.' she replies.

'Well, I've just been there for my first visit. It was after making friends with Pieter, from South Africa, who I met at the Observatory. He's a university lecturer. I heard the apostles Paul and John speak, along with Pieter himself, and some other wonderful people. It seems like I learned so much in such a short amount of time. I'll definitely be back there. So look out for me,' I say with a grin.

Finally we reach Parade Square and it's bustling with citizens and angels. At the far end of the square, the Hall of Honours stands out as an impressive twenty metre tall, rectangular building. This splendid crystal building is built with olive-green topaz and measures about sixty metres wide and 100 metres long. HALL OF HONOURS is inscribed on the large headstone over the main entrance, which stands open between two sturdy columns. Each of the three floors has large windows, and on the second storey the windows have balconies with gold railings.

Hannah and I go in through the shining pearl doors, which look like smaller versions of the gates found at the city gates. Inside, there's a sizeable reception hall. One of the many attendant angels directs us across to the guest room. Here we are each handed a golden sash to wear over our white robes. An angel helps me to place the sash over my head, ensuring it hangs correctly from my right shoulder and across to my left hip.

As I'm being dressed, the angel quietly tells me, 'This is the only time citizens are honoured to wear the golden sash. Only Messiah Jesus wears a sash like this one. You wear it to show everyone that the Lord shares his honour with you.'

I quickly find Hannah and as we wait to be called into the grand chamber we admire each other's appearance. I feel nervous with excitement. There are around a hundred other people in our group, including some children, all due to receive honours at the same time. I recognise several familiar faces among them.

Hannah whispers, 'Oh Jamie, isn't this exciting? I'm glad you're here with me; it's also a bit scary.'

Before I can reply, the double doors to the chamber are opened from the inside, by two radiant angels. All of us are escorted inside as a trumpet ensemble plays a short welcome fanfare.

I enter the grand chamber and immediately see an elevated, high-backed seat, carved from deep-red crystal and set in a private balcony facing the audience. I realise that this must be the Judgement Seat of Messiah. A quick scan of the vast rectangular hall reveals two massive tiered balconies, which extend around three sides of the hall. The chamber is filled from the ground floor arena to the top balcony with over two thousand citizens. Compared to other places I've visited in heaven, the atmosphere here is muted and rather reserved. Clearly, this is a serious occasion for everyone. I recall Pieter's comment that not everyone merits the same rewards. Some people will have achieved much for the kingdom of heaven; others will have done less.

Thoughts fly through my mind, about the warning given by the apostle Paul, in his letter to the church at Corinth. *"Each person's work will become evident; for the day will show it because it is to be revealed with fire, and the fire itself will test the quality of each person's work. Whoever's work remains, they will receive a reward."*

Hannah and I are soon shown to our red and white striped onyx benches, which look rather like posh church pews. Hannah is on the third row and I'm on the fifth. I look at the audience across the ground floor arena and spot several people I know. I can see Pieter and Ishran sat together - I think they've just recognised me. A little further back, I see Gramps and Grandma Minnie sitting with my great aunts, Annie and Alma, there's also my niece Karen. I then also recognise my Uncle Frank sat towards the back. Grandma gives me a little familiar wave with her hand. I'm really pleased to see everyone here.

Opposite us, and seated in rows, are a similar number of angels each holding small scrolls. I instantly recognise Thaniel and Jediah, but I realise this is not the best moment for me to wave across at them! The trumpets play a second fanfare and everyone stands to their feet, in expectant silence.

Over the special balcony to my left, a bright, thickening cloud appears. Within moments, Jesus Messiah appears and stands surrounded in shining glory, with two winged-cherubim on either side. A holy awesomeness fills the chamber, and I feel myself quiver. Jesus sits down on his Judgement Seat and high in the chamber a choir of angels begins to sing a hymn of praise to God. We continue to stand very still in an atmosphere of intense anticipation.

One of the angels standing opposite steps forward and the ceremony commences. Everyone quietly sits down. I figure that these angels must be the guardian angels of the citizens receiving their rewards. Their first task is to read the citation, which is written on a scroll for each person. Firstly the angel announces the person's name, along with their place of birth. The named individual then moves out of their row, steps forward and looks up at Jesus in the balcony.

One by one the people in our group are called forward to receive their honours. Each angel reads from the scroll and informs Jesus of the areas of service fulfilled by the individual. The commendations are based on their actions, spoken words and service for Messiah while on earth.

In these sacred moments, the words of Scripture ring out in my mind. *"Everyone will have to give account at the Judgement Seat of Messiah"*.

Each Christian is accountable for their service for God and we can expect to be rewarded accordingly. I'm reminded of the Olympic Games medal ceremonies when participants receive gold, silver or bronze. It only takes minutes to receive a prize, but the rewards of receiving an Olympic medal last a lifetime. The presentation of crowns in heaven symbolises the rewards given to each citizen for eternity.

As more people step forward, I realise that service for God takes many different forms. Some have served with national governments, while others have worked within their local communities. Some have been witnesses in the business world, and others have had professional vocations, such as teachers, accountants, nurses and social workers. Many have served in their homes raising families, while others have spent their lives meeting the needs of the poor. Some have worked in retail, some in administration and others in manufacturing. Finally there are those who have been called as pastors, evangelists, teachers and musicians in the church.

Each time the account is read out, attention is paid to the person's faithfulness to God's commands, to upright living and to the Gospel. The broader the areas of responsibility held by each individual - the greater the scope of judgement. I'm struck by the fact that the nature of the work we have done is of little concern. It's our faithfulness to God that counts. There's no condemnation here, no shame and no embarrassment. The Lord is pleased to honour his people.

I watch closely as Jesus receives the selected crown from one of the cherubim. The recipient then climbs the three steps to a small platform, in front of Messiah's balcony. Each person then bows their head toward the Lord, who leans forward over the balcony and places the crown on their head. The honoured citizen remains bowed for a few moments.

I also begin to notice, there are different kinds of crowns, and some citizens receive two or even three crowns. The depth of banding around the crown varies, as well as the type of ornamentation. The various crowns appear to reflect different aspects of service for God. In our group there are two people who have already received martyrs crowns, there's also mention of an eternal crown, a crown of joy, a crown of righteousness, a crown of glory and the crown of life.

'Jamie Ocklestone, Abingdon, England,'

I suddenly realise Thaniel is calling out my name. I get up, move to the end of my row, and step forward to look up into the eyes of the Lord Jesus. Those burning, searching eyes are full of grace and mercy.

Thaniel continues to read from the scroll, as I face towards the Lord. 'Your servant, Jamie, remained faithful to the gospel. His witness led to twenty three people becoming Christians. He loved to read and obey your word and kept himself pure from the deceit of the world.'

Then one of the cherubim asks me in a loud, clear voice, 'Is this a true account of your service for God?'

Without hesitation, I answer, 'Yes,' and turn my gaze back towards the brightness of Jesus Messiah.

The cherub then instructs me, 'Stand forward to receive your reward - a crown of righteousness and a crown of life.'

I move forward, climb the steps and bow my head. Jesus places the crown firmly on my head and then, to my amazement, presents a second crown. He smiles and says to me, 'Well done Jamie, my good and faithful servant.'

Elated, I carefully step down from the platform, bow again to the Lord and then turn to walk back to my place. Surely, nothing can mean more to me, than to hear 'well done' from the Lord. But my rejoicing must wait until everyone has received their honours.

After me a young boy, around twelve years of age, steps forward. He looks so smart, with his short black hair, his white robe and golden sash. I learn from the angel that his name is Tomas and he was born in Kells, Ireland. He receives a crown of glory. His citation mentions his service for God as a helper at a children's camp in Drewstown House. While there he shared the gospel with two of his young friends, who both become Christians. He returns to his seat wearing his crown, with a huge grin all over his face.

It's not long before Jediah, who I've already met, moves to the front and calls forward my friend.

'Hannah Prince, from Chicago, United States of America.'

She quickly slips out of the row and stands before the Lord. Jediah reads from the scroll.

'Since becoming a believer, at the age of eight years, Hannah has been a faithful witness, even though she was teased and bullied at school. She kept her heart pure before the Lord. She has used her gifts in music and drama to glorify God.'

Then the cherub asks her, 'Is this a true account of your service for God?'

Hannah replies, 'Yes Lord,' as she looks directly at Jesus.

The cherub then says to her, 'Stand forward to receive your reward - a crown of glory.'

She steps up to the platform and bows her head. Jesus gently positions the crown and says, 'Well done Hannah, my good and faithful servant.'

Hannah returns to her row in front of me. She looks radiant and everything about her says princess.

I'm a little surprised, when a group of five angels step forward to speak. In turn they call out the African names of Adebayo, Ngozi, Osaze, Adeola and Esosa. Each of them was born in Katsina State, northern Nigeria. Two men, a young boy and two women slowly step forward together, and stand in a line. Their joyful faces look to Jesus, as the citations are read out. Each citizen in turn receives from Jesus the martyrs' crown of life, before they file back to their seats on the front row. Images flash through my mind from the funeral service in Nigeria, which I watched in the Observatory.

Are these the ones who gave their lives in the service of Messiah? I ask myself. I'm sure they must be.

Among the final citizens receiving honours are a couple, who I recognise. I first saw them when they arrived in heaven with their young son, and then later at the Throne Room. They are announced by their guardian angels as, Sue and Marcus Johnson, from Perth, Australia. Their faithful service for God included hundreds of hours of voluntary work at the local Food Bank. This was a ministry in the name of Messiah to the poor of their city in Western Australia. They both receive a crown of righteousness.

After the final citation, the trumpet fanfare is played again and everyone stands in silence.

The cherub on the right of Jesus announces with a loud voice, 'All newly honoured citizens are invited as the King's guests to the Banqueting Hall. Please now take your places in the parade to Praise Pavilion.'

In full view of everyone, a cloud of shining glory envelops Messiah Jesus and the cherubim, and they disappear from view.

The atmosphere changes, as spontaneous clapping and loud shouts of praise break out across the auditorium. The angel choir then sings another resounding hymn of praise.

The guardian angels begin to exit the hall through the double doors, quickly followed by those of us who have received our crowns. As we leave the building, I discover a large procession is forming in Parade Square. There are thousands of citizens watching from all around the square, and the numbers are growing rapidly. The well-wishers who have just left the Hall of Honours are eager to watch what promises to be a pageant.

At the head of the parade are twelve pairs of angel trumpeters sitting on white horses. Just behind them there are several rows of angels in horse drawn chariots, around fifty altogether. Then there's a group of older men with crowns and wearing purple sashes around their white robes. We are positioned directly behind them. I hear someone near to me mention, 'twenty-four elders' and then I realise just who they are. I remember Ishran explaining all this to me, when I first watched the arrival of the newly honoured citizens at Praise Pavilion.

The trumpets play a short anthem before the heavy clatter of horses and chariots is heard, as they begin to move across the square at a steady pace. In no time we are all marching along in step together, as the crowds cheer and wave. As I look at the crowds watching the parade, I spot two ladies waving furiously at me. It's the two sisters, Edith and Ethel! I wave back at them. I'm so pleased to see them, and even more delighted they still recognise me after our brief chat by the river in Benjamin Street.

I think back to my arrival in heaven, when I found myself among some of these same people. So much was unknown and heaven was waiting to be discovered. Now, as we walk alongside each other again, everyone is happy and the whole atmosphere is full of celebration and joy.

Among all the cheering cries, I suddenly hear my name being called out loudly in unison.

'Jamie, Jamie over here!'

I look across to see my Uncle Frank, Aunts Annie and Alma, and Karen along with Gramps and Grandma all frantically waving to me from the front row of the crowd. I wave back.

'Great to see you all,' I shout, but I think my words are lost among the noise.

Hannah has somehow managed to join my row, and we walk side by side. Soon, we leave Parade Square and turn right along Joseph Street towards the city centre. Just at the corner, I spot Ishran and Pieter, who are calling out their greetings and waving wildly. It's impossible to hear what they're saying, as the cheering is so loud and the trumpets continue to play. I tap Hannah's shoulder and point them out. We both wave at them and see their smiles. With appreciative crowds lining both sides of the highway, we wave back at the onlookers while keeping in step with the procession.

A little further on, during a lull in the music, Hannah nudges me in the ribs, and as I look at her she laughs out loudly.

'Jamie, you do look rather funny wearing those two crowns.' She's obviously amused at my regal appearance.

'Yes, it feels strange to be wearing them.' I reply, 'but at the same time it's a real honour. To think Jesus Messiah himself placed these crowns on our heads. It's a token of his regard of us and especially for our faithfulness. I doubt I'll wear my crowns very often, but this occasion will never be forgotten.'

'Hannah, your crown really suits you. You're looking like a princess.' I tell her.

'Oh thank you Jamie,' she says with a sweet smile. 'You always say such kind things. I think the true rewards in heaven are the joys we have all being together, and the kindness others show toward us in such a beautiful place.'

I say to Hannah, 'Well, I'm so glad I made my relationship with God a priority and invested in eternity. I could easily have got totally involved in sport or making lots of money. But God kept these things in check. The kingdom of heaven always came first in my life.'

As we cross Miriam Avenue, the view of the canal is hidden behind the lines of waving crowds, but it's not long before we reach the city centre. Among the tall buildings the blare of the trumpets sounds louder than ever; the cheers and shouts of the watching crowds are relentless. Huge crowds line the eastern side of Throne Square as the parade crosses the shallow stream. We soon reach Judah Street and the towering, striped onyx walls of the amphitheatre, Praise Pavilion.

The leading angel horsemen and charioteers form a guard of honour at both sides of the southern entrance. From inside the arena there are three victorious trumpet blasts. Immediately, the newly honoured citizens follow the twenty-four elders through the passageway below the grandstand. The elders walk in pairs, while the rest of us advance in rows of five.

As we emerge into the bright stadium the welcome is overwhelming. Many thousands of citizens are on their feet cheering. We turn to our left to commence our lap of honour along the golden, oval walkway. The vast, angelic choir in the upper grandstand is singing. The atmosphere is electric and, for a few moments, I imagine I must be dreaming.

All around the central area of the arena I can see an assortment of coloured flags being waved. My mind goes back to my first visit to the pavilion, when the flags were paraded in from each of the twelve gates. I look at Hannah beside me, she too is overcome with emotion, and tears are streaming down her face.

We reach the orchestra on the western side of the pavilion. The musicians are playing a rousing military-style march, with the crowd clapping along with the beat. Our whole company continue walking around the far northern end of the arena, until we reach Jesus Messiah, who's standing in the royal balcony on the east side. Facing the Lord we join the honourable elders and kneel down as a group. Carefully we remove our crowns and lay them in front of us; the gold glints in my eyes. I gladly give my honour back to God; I know without a doubt that he alone deserves everything.

As the pavilion becomes silent, there's a great sense of awe as many hearts worship the Lord. In these moments, I watch the first signs of the glory cloud appear around the royal box, floating like wisps of mist. The cloud thickens and brightens as Jesus and the cherubim slowly disappear from sight. Just as on my first visit, I remain kneeling in God's holy presence. There's nothing more I can do to show my thankfulness to God. God is my reward. It is he who is faithful and I put my trust in his precious promises.

Eventually we are joined in the arena by Thaniel and Jediah.

Thaniel says, 'Jamie, there's something I need to tell you. My guardianship of you is soon coming to an end. I've watched over the whole of your life. No one rejoiced more than I did, when you turned your life over to Messiah Jesus. I'll always be here for you and I know we will often meet up. There is just one more place to which I must bring you. I want you to see Angel Headquarters but first there's the celebration!'

'Celebration?' I ask, 'I thought this was the celebration.'

'Yes, but you've been invited to the banquet,' Thaniel says.

'Of course, the banquet,' I repeat.

Jediah turns to Hannah and myself and says with a rare smile, 'And the guardian angels get to go too. It's our last official time with you. Hannah you'll love the banquet. It's the most wonderful party ever.'

Hannah replies, 'It sounds fabulous and I'm really glad we'll all be together.'

THE BANQUET

We attract plenty of attention among the thousands of citizens, as we leave Praise Pavilion and walk back along Judah Street. Still wearing our gold crowns and bright golden sashes, Hannah and I stand out from the crowd. Several people offer us their congratulations. We also receive many more smiles than usual, and even get a few waves from passers-by. Thaniel and Jediah soon catch up and walk with us into Throne Square.

It's been a rollercoaster experience ever since we arrived at the Hall of Honours and received our crowns. Then we joined the parade through the city centre to the pavilion. The welcome we received there was totally overwhelming; something I'll never forget. I'm now really looking forward to the banquet to which we've been invited.

Thaniel informs us, 'As your guardian angels we escort you to the banquet and then, along with the other angels, help to serve the guests.'

I'm really pleased our guardian angels will be joining Hannah and myself at the banquet, as they are such great friends.

As soon as we arrive at Throne Square, I see two familiar figures waving at us. It's the first time I've seen them wearing their golden crowns.

'Look, it's Gramps and Grandma Minnie.' I call out.

As we all meet up, I hug both of them in turn and say, 'Gramps and Grandma, I'm having such an incredible time with my friend and the angels. We're on our way to the banquet after receiving our crowns.'

'Yes, we know,' Gramps replies, as Grandma nods. 'We saw you in the pavilion and felt so proud of you and your service for Jesus. We also cried with tears of joy, when the account of your life was read out at the crowning ceremony.'

'Oh, this is my friend Hannah.' I say, pointing her out with my hand. 'And these are our guardian angels, Thaniel and Jediah,' I add, as both angels smile and nod politely.

Gramps and Grandma give all three of them a welcome embrace.

Grandma looks at me and says, 'Well Jamie, we've also been invited to the banquet, which is why we're wearing our crowns. As the area around the pavilion was so busy, Gramps suggested we wait here by the steps on the square until you arrive. We thought you would be heading in this direction.'

I'm always pleased to see Gramps and Grandma and feel really happy they'll be joining us. The plaza is full of activity as we walk across its blue paving. Turning right into Naphtali Street, we get split up into two groups. I'm walking with Gramps and Thaniel, and Hannah is just ahead talking with Grandma and Jediah. Looking around at Naphtali Street, I can't help but notice the rich colours of the balconied apartments along both sides of the highway. Almost all the buildings are themed with the warm shades of amethyst; burgundy, purple, mauve and violet.

We soon cross the canal at the Miriam Avenue junction and begin to look for the Banqueting Hall. All of a sudden, I feel a hand on my shoulder. I stop, and turn around to see who it is.

'Pieter and Ishran!' I shout out with excitement, causing Gramps and Thaniel to glance back.

I put my arms around my friends; still unsure who touched me.

Pieter says, 'We hoped to catch up with you, because both of us received invites to the banquet too!'

'We saw you taking part in the parade to the pavilion.' Ishran adds.

I introduce everyone to Pieter and Ishran, 'Guys, this is my grandfather, I call him Gramps. Also, this is Thaniel who's my guardian angel. Then just up ahead is my grandma, along with my friend, Hannah and her guardian angel, Jediah.'

I'm used to seeing Pieter wearing his crown, but then I realise Ishran is also wearing his crown.

I ask Thaniel, 'Do all the guests at the banquet wear crowns? And what about the citizens who haven't received a crown?'

He replies, 'Banquets are held for all new citizens, even those who have no crown to wear. All the newly honoured citizens also wear their golden sashes. The other invited guests, who have crowns, are encouraged to wear them for this special occasion.'

Pieter adds, 'The angels have always enjoyed God's honour and glory; they are sent to the banquet to serve. They take much pleasure in helping God's people to achieve their own crowns, through their service on earth.'

We quickly join Hannah, Jediah and Grandma, who have stopped to enjoy the scene. My first view of the Banqueting Hall is breathtaking.

This must be one of the most beautiful places in heaven. In the centre of a formal garden, which measures around 100 metres square, stands a large ornamental conservatory made from amethyst crystal. The thirty-metre-square conservatory looks like a palace made with lilac-tinted glass. On each side there are three wide arches, which provide easy access and a clear view inside. Surrounding the Banqueting Hall, there's a series of amethyst columns from which purple and white drapes hang horizontally. The loosely twisted drapes criss-cross white crystal tables, which are laden with fruit. More than fifty tables with benches are positioned uniformly around the garden. Each corner of the garden has a tall water fountain, which has been carved from fuchsia-pink crystal. At either side of the fountains, stand a pair of burgundy-coloured pergolas surrounded by palm trees. Although the overall size of the Banqueting Hall is much smaller than I expected, the venue looks magnificent.

Slowly, we all walk towards the Banqueting Hall and join the other guests who are arriving. The gentle music of flute and harp can be heard coming from inside the conservatory.

Hannah says to everyone, 'Oh I love that tune; it's called "Majesty". It's one of my favourite pieces and reminds me of Mozart. We sometimes perform it in the village square.'

As I approach the tables set between the columns, I inhale the fragrance of lavender.

An attendant angel steps forward to greet us.

'Welcome to the Banqueting Hall, please follow me,' he instructs us.

Walking beneath the overhead drapes, we pass the first row of tables; some guests are already seated. The angel leads us along the path, around the outside of the conservatory. As we pass the arches I get my first glimpse inside. The conservatory is about seven metres high, and at the south side is seated a chamber orchestra. There are about fifteen musicians of various ages, along with their instruments; violins, harps and flutes. At the opposite end of the crystal chamber on a small platform, a golden throne is positioned behind the top table. The table is arranged in a u-shape with twelve high-backed chairs positioned on each side.

Thaniel tells me, 'Those seats are reserved for the honourable elders.'

The long tables are decorated with flower arrangements and bowls of exotic-looking fruit. Around an extra-large table, placed in the centre of the conservatory, angels are busily bringing goblets of wine and carrying platters of bread and cake. Several of the elders, recognisable by their purple sashes, have already arrived; they chat and laugh enthusiastically among themselves. I notice among them the apostle John, who I saw at the University, and also hear a mention of Joseph.

All eight of us are shown to our table on the west side of the garden. We have a clear view of the orchestra through the crystal arches. Four guests are already sitting at our table, which is laid out for twelve. They look up and smile; I immediately recognise two of them and feel very pleased.

It takes a few moments for us to decide where everyone is sitting. The table is filled with bowls of delicious fruit, which looks so mouth-watering. The fruit includes; grapes, apples, pears, strawberries, plums and peaches. There's also some exotic-looking fruit I've never seen before.

Before I sit down, I look across the table at the familiar face of my friend from the Library.

'Lucas, how good to see you again. It's great that you can meet more of my family and friends, who are here at the banquet.'

Lucas looks at me and says, 'I was really looking forward to seeing who else would be sitting at this table. I've been to the banquet many times before, and I always enjoy catching up with people I know and also making new friends.'

Once we're all seated, I introduce myself, and quickly point out Thaniel, Hannah and Jediah, Ishran and my grandparents, Richard and Minnie.

I explain to everyone how I came to meet Lucas. 'I met Lucas on my very first to the Library, or rather he met me. He took time out to show me around the Library's many rooms. This is the same Lucas, also known as Luke, who wrote the Gospel and the Acts of the Apostles. He spends a lot of time in the Library, so do watch out for him.'

Gramps replies, 'Lucas, it's a real honour to meet you. I feel we are going to have a great time here together.'

The other guest I recognise is the young boy Tomas, from Ireland, who attended the same crowning ceremony as Hannah and myself. He's wearing his crown and still smiling.

Looking across the table at him, I give a little wave and trying to be friendly say, 'Hello Tomas, my name's Jamie. We were at the same crowning ceremony; it's so good to see you here.'

Tomas looks across at me and says, 'Hi,' and quickly glances around at the rest of the group.

I tell him, 'I was really pleased to hear about your story Tomas. You must be thrilled to get your crown?'

'Yes, I was. But I offered it straight back to Jesus in the pavilion because I love him so much,' Tomas replies with enthusiasm. Then he adds, pointing with his thumb to the angel beside him, 'Oh, and this is Finbar, my angel and best friend. It was Finbar who told me to keep my crown to honour Jesus Messiah, so I'm sure fine with that,' he adds with another big smile.

I ask Finbar, 'Do you know Thaniel and Jediah?'

Finbar nods with a look of recognition and replies, 'Oh yes, we angels go back a long way together.'

Grandma then turns to the other guest, an older lady with a serene smile, who's wearing two crowns.

'Hello, my dear, how nice it is to be joining you at this table. My name's Minnie, what's yours?'

We all look toward the lady, who's sat at the far end of the table.

'Hello Minnie...and everyone else,' she responds while looking all around, 'I'm Audrey.'

'Hello Audrey,' We all chime out at the same moment, and then laugh loudly together at the sound of our voices.

She smiles back and then reveals her link with my family.

'Jamie, you don't recognise me; I'm a friend of your mother, Margaret, and I also know your Uncle Frank. We were all in the same year at school in Oxford. In fact a few years later, it was Frank who introduced Margaret to his brother Edward, who later became your dad. After teacher training college, I got married and my husband and I became missionaries in Kenya, where we served God for many years in a secondary school. Your mum and I wrote to each other regularly. You might remember her referring to me as Audrey Longstaff. I was at the Hall of Honours for the crowning ceremony and the moment your name was read out, I instantly realised who you were. Shortly afterwards I received an invitation to the banquet.'

'Audrey Longstaff?' I repeat slowly. 'Yes, I do remember mum talking about you, and didn't you always send us a Christmas card?' I ask.

She answers, 'That's right. But most important of all was the praying. Your mum and dad faithfully prayed for our work; we saw many young Kenyans become Christians.'

I get up, walk around the table and give Audrey a big hug and say, 'I'm so glad you are here with us all.'

Pieter says, 'This is a wonderful story, especially as I love the nations of Africa so much; South Africa was my home country.'

Our banqueting table is now complete with nine citizens and three guardian angels. On my left hand side are Gramps, Grandma, Hannah and Jediah, and on my right side is Thaniel. Opposite me from left to right are Ishran, Pieter, Lucas, young Tomas, Audrey and Finbar.

There are twelve more tables, just like ours, on each side of the crystal conservatory and the now the whole Banqueting Hall looks just about full. With almost 600 guests the atmosphere is exuberant. There's much noisy conversation with shrieks of laughter all around us. One of the attendant angels places a large, golden goblet of red wine in the centre of our table.

All conversation is then interrupted by the orchestra's loud playing of a baroque-style fanfare. After the final notes, all the angels stand up, quickly followed by the guests. Everyone remains quiet as our eyes turn towards the conservatory and we look toward the top table. Through the thin crystal walls, we can see all twenty-four elders stood at their tables on either side of the throne. The orchestra is also on its feet.

As we watch, the glory cloud of heaven fills the conservatory with soft, white light. Through the thin haze we see the Lord, Messiah Jesus appear. He stands in dazzling radiance, at the head of the top table in front of his throne; two cherubim are with him. Jesus is wearing his crown, a brilliant white robe with a bright golden sash.

The Messiah reaches out both hands to lift the goblet of wine from the table in front of him. He holds it high and confidently proclaims, 'This is the fruit of the vine; I now drink it with you in My Father's kingdom.'

Jesus then lowers the goblet, tilts it toward his lips and takes a slow sip of the wine.

Breaking the silence again, he says in a loud clear voice, 'Take this wine before you; share the communion blessing of the kingdom of heaven.'

He passes the goblet to the cherub on his right, and then raises his arms as a sign of blessing. The cherub walks around the outer edge of the top table and faces the elders. From the centre of the table, he passes the goblet across to each one in turn.

When all the elders have sipped the wine, the cherub returns the goblet to Jesus. Then the Messiah says, 'My honoured citizens, you may now drink the fruit of the vine set on the tables in front of you.'

Jesus sits down on his throne to preside over the banquet and both cherubim step back to stand behind his throne. The orchestra resumes its music, with strings and harps playing softly in the background.

All the guests sit down at their tables and Thaniel and Jediah slip away to carry out their serving duties. Finbar lifts the communal goblet of wine from our table and passes it first to Audrey, who closes her eyes while she takes a sip and then hands it back. Then it's my turn to receive the cup. I taste the light, fruity wine and it quickly dissolves in my mouth, which leaves a rich, warm lingering flavour. I then pass the goblet to Gramps, who shares it with Grandma and Hannah. Finbar receives the wine from Hannah and passes it to Ishran, Pieter, Lucas and last of all Tomas, who drinks the wine and briefly bows his head.

I think back to regular Sunday communion services in my church, when we thought about the sacrifice of Jesus on the cross. It was an important reminder of the shedding of his blood for our sins and the hope of eternal life. I have begun to 'drink the cup' again in heaven as a celebration of the kingdom of God and the fellowship shared with brothers and sisters.

Jediah returns to our table carrying two platters of sliced baguettes, which he carefully sets down and then leaves without a saying a word. The thin sliced, dark-brown bread smells deliciously aromatic, and has a shiny crust covered with tiny yellow seeds. Pieter passes the platter of bread across the table towards me and Gramps. I pick up a slice and am surprised just how wafer-light it feels. Taking my first bite, I discover a crisp, honey-flavoured texture, which soon melts in my mouth leaving a deliciously sweet taste. In no time the slice is consumed.

Gramps turns to me and asks, 'Well, Jamie, what's the verdict of heaven's bread?'

'Absolutely delicious,' I immediately reply. After a pause I continue, 'Every day the Israelites gathered from the ground their manna from heaven to make bread. I've often wondered what it tasted like and now I've a pretty good idea.'

Gramps smiles and says, 'It came from heaven, so it must have been good.'

Thaniel then appears carrying two trays of cakes, piled high on small plates.

'Here are the sweet breads,' he announces as he places each tray at either end of the table. Another angel brings two more goblets of wine.

Ishran lifts the wine goblet nearest to him and offers it to Pieter. He takes a long sip and then passes it round the table, as we each take another drink. The velvety-smooth, fruity wine is delightful to the palate, and perfectly matches the joy I feel in my heart.

Lucas says, 'The banquet celebrates all that God has provided for us through his son, Jesus Messiah. The Lord God has given him the throne of his ancestral father, King David. He now reigns over the house of Jacob forever, and of his kingdom there shall be no end.'

Pieter responds, 'It's by God's grace that those of us, who were not born Jews, have been given the right to enter this kingdom. Jew and non-Jew, we have all entered God's promised blessing.'

Hannah then adds, 'Here in heaven, we experience the beauty and harmony of God's kingdom. It's our delight to accept his authority in every aspect of life. Only in heaven, do we see the big picture of God's eternal purposes. On earth our view was restricted and time spent there was very short.'

Tomas then asks, 'Would anyone else like one of those tasty-looking cakes?'

We all laugh at his innocent question and Tomas grins back.

Audrey lifts a plate of cakes and says to Tomas, 'Please take one.'

Tomas takes a moment to choose, selecting one of the raisin cakes and takes a healthy bite; he clearly enjoys the taste. Audrey then offers me a cake.

My small cake is flavoured with lemon and almond. The soft, buttery texture soon dissolves leaving a zesty after-taste.

All I say is, 'Scrumptious!'

Ishran eats his cake and suddenly says, 'I'm sure mine has cinnamon flavour. My mother called it Dalchini. I never thought I would taste this again, especially in heaven!'

I catch a glimpse of Jesus laughing, as he engages in jovial conversation with the elders. The banquet is being shared by everyone, and it really does feel as though we're all eating at the one big table.

Ishran continues, 'Heaven is such a joy-filled place. If only we knew more about heaven while on earth, I'm sure we would all serve God with constant obedience. The trouble is that sometimes we want to hold on to earthly things. But the real gain is only found in heaven, where our reward lasts forever.'

Pieter says, 'I'm so glad I set my heart to fully serve God. Even though my time on earth was suddenly cut short, my service for God continues for ever. Nothing I gave up on earth was wasted. I agree with Ishran; to be with God in heaven is always better.'

Grandma joins the conversation as we drink more wine and enjoy the sweet breads and cakes.

She says, 'Gramps and I had a wonderful family on earth; we spent many happy times together. Christmas, Easter and birthdays were cause for great joy. But anxiety, about the lives of one or more of our family members, was never far away. There was sometimes illness, accidents, unemployment, bullying at school, divorce, unpleasant neighbours, and financial worries and so the list went on. Gramps and I set our hearts on following God, always putting him first and making his kingdom our priority. Now I know, without a doubt, heaven is our true destination. We may suffer loss and hardship on earth, but that is such a small price to pay to share eternal life with God.'

Gramps adds, 'Yes, what really counts is not our achievement on earth, but our eternal destiny with God.'

'Amen, to that,' says Lucas.

Audrey looks toward Gramps and says, 'What's so important for me, Richard, is our worship of God. To truly know him, serve him and honour him during our life on earth. Knowing the presence of God is our preparation for eternity. Now I understand so much more about the promise of eternal life, which Jesus gave us. The truth is, when we put our faith in Messiah Jesus and welcome him as Lord and Saviour, we receive eternal life.'

Gramps smiles and nods his head in agreement with Audrey.

'Anyone for fruit?' asks Hannah.

There's such a variety of fruit set out in the bowls in front of us. Tomas chooses some grapes, Lucas picks up a couple of strawberries and Audrey selects an apple. Gramps and Grandma both lift pears, Ishran selects a peach and I decide on a juicy plum, which thankfully is stone-less.

Conversation around the table is put on pause, as we eat our fruit and absorb the sweet and succulent flavours. In heaven, the sight of fruit on the trees and food on the table creates a curious sense of appetite. Eternal life is, of course, not dependent on food. No one gets hungry or ever feels thirsty. Our spiritual bodies have no need of food and none is digested. However the tasty flavour of the food and drink in heaven is something every citizen relishes, especially here at the banquet.

I ask Lucas, 'Please tell us about the promised marriage supper of the Lamb?'

Lucas pauses before he replies, 'The great marriage supper of the Lamb is yet to take place. It will be at the end of the earth age when God's purposes are fulfilled. The resurrection the dead and the Great Judgement must first take place. Jesus Messiah will be finally joined by his bride, the church. All who believe will be together here in heaven's city, the New Jerusalem. Everyone will be invited to the marriage celebration meal. Afterwards the city will be relocated from heaven to the new earth where Messiah will reign forever with his bride.'

'But where will the marriage meal take place? Which building is large enough?' I ask.

Lucas replies, 'The supper will take place across heaven's entire city. Every community, every avenue and every street will be filled with feasting and celebration. What we experience at the Banqueting Hall will take place everywhere. The angels will serve us and there will be plenty of food and drink for everyone.'

Tomas says, with his youthful enthusiasm, 'Wow, I for one, can't wait for the marriage meal.'

Audrey adds, 'How I look forward to the final reunion, when we're joined together with all those who have truly loved and served God.'

Hannah nods her agreement, saying, 'Yes, every family member, who has received Jesus as Messiah, will be here with us forever. That will be incredibly wonderful.'

Pieter agrees, 'Yes, it's what we all long for. The kingdom of heaven will be complete. Messiah Jesus and his bride will rule God's kingdom.'

As Pieter speaks, the sound of the orchestra's fanfare fills the air. We all stand and watch as the dense glory-cloud returns to the conservatory to receive Jesus and the cherubim, leaving an empty throne. He must return to his place in the Throne Room, at his Father's right hand.

The atmosphere soon changes and the banquet comes to an end. The orchestra continues to play its chamber music, while guests begin to make their way out through the gardens. Conversations linger at many of the tables, as guests sip their final drinks and share round the remaining cakes.

Thaniel and Jediah return to the table, just as we are preparing to leave.

Thaniel gives us instructions, 'Hannah, Tomas and Jamie, it's now time to return your golden sashes. I'll take them back to the Hall of Honours.'

With great care, all three of us remove our crowns. We are then helped, by our guardian angels, to take off the sashes from over our heads. Thaniel gathers the sashes together and carries them over his arm. With our crowns back in place, we all leave the Banqueting Hall.

I stop briefly to admire the beautiful sprinkling fountain in the corner. It makes me think of the stream that flows from God's throne, along Benjamin Street and across the city, feeding the canals and fountains of heaven. It's just like God's rule that extends to every place and continues for ever.

We've little more to say to each another as we all walk back along Naphtali Street. The banquet has been a rich feast of food and friendship that we've shared together. I now feel so much part of heaven and, as a citizen, I look forward to the future and all that God has planned.

On reaching Throne Square, I say my goodbyes to Audrey, Lucas, Pieter, Tomas, Ishran and Hannah, as well as the angels.

Thaniel says, 'Jamie, remember, I've another place to show you. It's Angel HQ. Meet me again here in Throne Square.'

I reply, 'Of course I will. That will be brilliant. See you soon.'

Leaving the square with Gramps and Grandma, we walk back along Issachar Street to our apartments.

ANGEL HEADQUARTERS

Seeing angels flying overhead, in both small and large groups, has become a common sight. It's rather like watching fluffy, white clouds floating by on a summer's day on earth. All angels appear to be able to fly and can travel instantaneously if required. I've also seen thousands of angels walking among the citizens, and even watched some riding their chariots. Although the cherubim and seraphim have visible wings, I've only observed them either standing as guards or gathered inside the Throne Room.

Angels are always visible in heaven busy serving God in different ways. Although there are millions of angels, each one seems to be given a unique role or specific assignment. Who better than my guardian angel, Thaniel, to show me around Angel Headquarters.

As I arrive in Throne Square, Thaniel is waiting for me beside the plaza steps. I don't think he's been there long.

'Hi Thaniel, I'm really excited about our visit to angel HQ,' I tell him, as we hug each other.

We cross the stream at the entrance to Benjamin Street and set off toward Dan Street.

I'm noticing many more angels around at the moment; this could be simply because of where we're going. A surprising thing I've discovered about angels is that they are not as sociable as citizens. Unlike people, they never glance from side to side to observe what's going on around them. They are always so intent on their purposes, with absolute concentration and dedication and with their faces always set forward. Their sense of focus and mission is extreme. Although angels are polite and helpful they do not generally offer friendship, except for our guardian angels.

It's my first time in the north east area of the city centre and on reaching Dan Street I'm struck by the clean, fresh look of misty-white crystal used in the mansion blocks. The white glassy walls reflect the bright gold of the highway.

All around us, hundreds of angels are streaming back towards Angel Headquarters. Very soon we reach the headquarters, which is built in its own grounds close to the highway. Facing us is a formidable-looking building made from white crystal; it's around twenty metres high and 120 metres wide. Two broad, golden driveways lead up to the ten-metre-wide, twin gates, which form the grand double entrance.

Both driveways are full of returning angels, including around a dozen horse-drawn chariots on the right-hand side. Very little conversation is taking place among them and any exchanges appear brief and to the point. This is clearly a place of industrious activity.

'Why are there two sets of gates into the HQ?' I ask Thaniel.

'Oh, that's because the work of the angels is always divided between heaven and earth. Angels on assignments in the city of heaven return through the entrance on the left. The other entrance is for angels who have served on the earth,' he responds.

The upper section of the building has a long row of narrow windows, and the roof is adorned with a series of lookout towers. Angel HQ appears to have extensive grounds to the rear, which are enclosed by a four-metre-high white wall on either side of the building.

Thaniel turns to me and says, 'I'm taking you to the citizens' gallery, where you will be able to see for yourself what takes place inside.'

'I'm so pleased we are allowed to go inside,' I reply.

We join several angels and walk through the left entrance. Once inside, I follow Thaniel as he escorts me round to the side of the building. We enter a small doorway leading to a spiral staircase, which we start to climb. It seems to go on forever. Finally, we reach the top and Thaniel leads me through a narrow doorway. It emerges into a crowded gallery, with three long rows of seats overlooking a great hall. We manage to find space along the front row, which offers us a real bird's-eye-view of proceedings.

On the ground floor below is a large gathering of angels. They are seated in rows and facing an arched pulpit standing three metres above the ground. The pulpit has been beautifully carved from white crystal. On either side of the pulpit are two small balconies with six angel trumpeters stood in readiness. I can't help noticing that the trumpeters to our left are holding small piccolo trumpets, whereas the angels on the right side are holding standard-sized trumpets.

Directly below each balcony is an enclosed pew where six angels on each side are stood facing each other as they wait.

I ask Thaniel in almost a whisper, 'Why are there two lots of trumpeters and two groups of angels, on either side of the pulpit?'

He quietly gives me his explanation, 'It's because of the dual nature of their work in heaven and on earth. The high pitch of the piccolo trumpets on the left heralds an assignment here in the city of heaven. But when the standard trumpets on the right are heard, it announces a mission on earth.'

'So who are the angels who stand waiting in the pews?' I then ask.

Thaniel replies, 'These are ruling angels who each have great authority over thousands of other angels.'

'This all sounds very organised. Is there a hierarchy among the angels?' I enquire.

'Most definitely,' Thaniel replies, 'As angels we all have different roles and tasks to perform. It's been like this from the beginning. You've seen for yourself the cherubim and the seraphim in the Throne Room. Those winged angelic beings are permanently assigned to wait in the presence of God. The seraphim are positioned to cover the throne, while the cherubim guard the base of the throne. Whenever Jesus Messiah appears in public places, he always has the cherubim beside him. Of course, the cherubim are also appointed to guard each of the twelve gates of heaven. '

Just at that moment, a powerful looking angel emerges through a door behind the pulpit. Immediately the piccolo trumpets are raised and the six angels sound out in unison a short fanfare. In the balcony below, the ruling angels instantly turn to face the messenger angel now stood above them in the pulpit.

With a loud voice the messenger declares, 'The changing of the gates is now. I call for choirs on high, I call for trumpeters on the walls and I call for guides and escorts to take their positions until further notice.'

The ruling angels, in the pew for heaven, suddenly vanish, and new angels quickly file in and replace them.

I ask Thaniel, 'Who is the angel giving the instructions?

Thaniel replies, 'He's one of the seven archangels who stand in front of the throne. They are the government ministers of the kingdom, who receive God's commands and execute his wishes without question. They deliver divine instructions directly from the Throne Room.'

'What other work in heaven is given to the angels?' I ask.

Thaniel answers, 'Guardian angels are commissioned to escort new arrivals and welcome citizens into heaven. Just as I was sent to greet you. The moment a Christian dies, their spirit goes to heaven. In the blink of an eye, each person is transformed into their heavenly body. They are immediately clothed by their guardian angels with new white robes. All signs of sickness, disability and the effects of ageing are gone. Unbelievers must wait for God's Judgement Day. Thousands of angels are assigned to sing in the vast choirs at each entrance gate. That's what the call we just heard was about.'

He continues, 'Angels also are given important roles in praise and worship, particularly in Praise Pavilion and also in the Throne Room. Other angels are given tasks in the Library, to help with the work of maintaining the written records.'

Thaniel adds, 'There's also an army of angels who care for babies. It's the angels who carry the babies into heaven. In every village community you find beautifully designed nurseries. Yes, even babies and toddlers have special places in heaven, which are filled with love and care. Little ones with bright shining eyes, who wave their hands and kick their legs, while others roll and crawl. In these special havens, there's no pain, no crying or sorrow, but plenty of smiles with gentle music from flute and harp and the sweetest of songs.'

'What about the older children?' I ask.

Thaniel says, 'In each neighbourhood there are angels who constantly entertain the children. Often they are taken together on trips to the parks, to Praise Pavilion and to the Library. They also play games, share stories, sing and dance together. It's a wonderful environment. Angels also ensure that newly arrived parents are always reunited with their own children, as soon as possible.'

Another trumpet fanfare echoes around the HQ; this time it's a call to earth.

The archangel makes the announcement with urgency, 'Warrior angels are summoned. I call for the angel horsemen to assist the church in Macedonia. God has heard the prayers of his people in Skopje, a church that is small but united. He declares a great advance for the kingdom of God. Go fulfil this purpose and reach all those who shall inherit salvation.'

Two of the six ruling angels in the pew disappear and are quickly replaced by two others.

I ask Thaniel, 'What happens next?'

He smiles back and says, 'The warrior angels immediately leave heaven and take up their positions over the hills surrounding city. They hold back the forces of darkness, while the Spirit of God moves among his people. There will be a season of spiritual harvest and answered prayer for the church in Macedonia.'

I'm really impressed with the speed at which God answers the prayers of his people. It feels as though there's a "tipping point" in prayer. The angels who stand before God, in the Throne Room, hold out their golden bowls waiting for them to be filled with the prayers of the saints. There appears to be a moment when the bowls begin to overflow and this releases divine intervention; often with angels being sent directly to earth.

While visiting the Observatory with Pieter I remember seeing how the angels responded to the cry of the martyrs in Nigeria. I now appreciate they had been specially assigned to the Observatory. Their task was to watch and wait for the opportunity to respond to the need. I want to find out more about this.

'Thaniel, are angels sent to watch events and places on earth?' I ask.

'Why yes, they are,' Thaniel replies without hesitation. 'Countless numbers of angels are spread across the world, and their work is to observe and to report. When you went to the Library, didn't you see the angels writing up their reports about what they witnessed while on earth? Angels are active in so many places, but usually they remain well hidden from view. Sometimes angels are watching when people offer hospitality to friends and strangers, even appearing dressed as strangers in human form. Angels watch over church gatherings, outreaches and missions of mercy. Other angels accompany those who serve God in travelling ministries, such as evangelists and apostles and prophets. Angels also watch over children and youth, as they witness at school or college.

Whatever the angels see and hear is recorded in heaven. Many of these records are presented as evidence in the Hall of Honours, when crowns and rewards and given. The lives of citizens and their service for God are judged on the basis of these records. All believers must stand to give an account of their words and actions.'

'What about angels sent as special messengers to the earth? I ask inquisitively.

Thaniel replies, 'It's rare for God to commission an angel to speak on earth, especially when he has already sent his own son. Remember, Messiah Jesus himself is the Word of God, and God has sent the Holy Spirit to help people hear and understand his word. But there have also been occasions when an angel has been sent. Gabriel, one of the seven archangels, has visited earth the most. Archangels are sent directly from the throne of God. The archangel, Michael has also been sent several times to assist the nation of Israel, when facing massive opposition from satanic powers.'

He adds, 'I remember when God sent an angel to release the apostle Peter from prison. I was also among the legions of angels who were poised in heaven, ready to assist Jesus during his earthly ministry, should he have asked for help from his Father, God. It was an archangel who spoke with the apostle John in a vision, and led him on his journey in heaven.'

'What's really important to know is that God alone commissions his angels. Angels know that only instructions which come from God's throne are legitimate. Angels are absolutely obedient. They never deviate and they always fulfil the tasks they are given. As angels we are also extremely focussed on what we do. The only time you are likely to see an angel smile is when he returns to heaven having completed his mission. Although Jamie, you often make me smile!'

Another blast from the standard trumpets gets everyone's attention. The archangel continues to commission the angels.

'I call for the angel of deliverance, to rescue adults and children, who are exiles from North Africa on board a small ship drifting in the Mediterranean.'

An angel from the right hand side immediately leaves the pew.

Thaniel says to me, 'Once again, it's the prayers of God's people, which have reached his throne. Here, God is showing his love and mercy to these families, who probably face drowning unless immediate help comes to them.'

I respond, 'Thaniel, let me ask you a personal question. When I was dying from cancer and my family and church prayed for me, why wasn't the angel sent?'

Thaniel pauses, 'Jamie my friend, I was ready to respond but the call was not given. It was your time to serve God in heaven. The prayers of your family and church would surely have reached the Throne Room. God alone determines the length of each person's days on earth. For God to act, it must be his will that matches with the prayers that are offered. Despite the sorrow and grief, the Lord brought great comfort to your family and church. I'm confident that they are now serving God with greater love and compassion - even though you were taken from them.'

'Come on, Jamie, let me take you round the rest of Angel HQ,' says Thaniel as he stands up.

I follow him back along the row of onlookers and leave the gallery by climbing a white spiral staircase. Half-way up I manage to get a brief look out of one of the narrow windows overlooking the square. From up here, it seems as if even more angels are arriving below us. In the distance, I see a long procession of angel charioteers, who are returning along Dan Street and cheered on by the crowds.

Catching up with Thaniel, along a narrow corridor, we reach an outer balcony, which overlooks the rear grounds of the HQ's main building. I'm stunned by what I see. To my left, there are literally thousands of angels stood in their golden chariots, which are harnessed to fine white horses. Angels and horses are ready for action; they stand almost motionless. Fully prepared for the word of command, the ranks of charioteers stretch back as far as I can see; the full number is impossible to count.

Positioned next to the charioteers is a vast army of angel horsemen. Their stallions wait with as much patience and control as they can exercise. I hear frequent snorts in the air as the horses prepare for action. Their riders carry silver shields and swords, drawn and ready for combat. These elite divisions look supremely capable and eager to serve their Lord God.

Suddenly, the captain of the host sitting astride his great stallion, and dressed in his smart white robe and bright yellow sash, shouts a command, 'For God and his kingdom.'

One thousand horsemen are instantly despatched and begin moving forward. Gathering pace with a thundering gallop, they quickly turn to the left only and disappear beyond the green fields.

'How I love to see them leave,' says Thaniel, as he turns to me on the balcony, 'It is a most thrilling sight. They will do battle in the lower heavens of the earth against evil forces, and in God's name will be victorious. There have been many battles in the past and there will be great battles to be fought in the future.'

We hear a second shout. 'For God and his kingdom.' This time it's declared by the leader of the charioteers. As the angels flick the reins, each row of horse-drawn chariots moves off and wheels round sharply to the left. Like a swathe of flaming fire tearing across the savannah, they follow the horsemen and soon vanish from sight.

In front of us, the remaining armies move forward to take up their positions of readiness. To our far right, stand row after row of soldier-angels, who are ready and waiting for service. There are about one hundred in each row. Among them is a group of around 300 trumpeters - the gleam of their golden trumpets is dazzling.

Thaniel nudges me and says, 'When I'm not with you, I'm alongside my fellow angels. I wait for my instructions over there. Sometimes I work with just a few angels and other times with many. Each time I complete my task, I return here to HQ and file my report.'

'Do you report everything?' I ask.

'No, only the main details. Let me show you where the reports on angelic activity are given and stored.'

We pass several other citizens, who are watching the same scenes from the balcony. At the far end, we walk down a flight of steps and reach a gallery overlooking a large rectangular hall. This room looks very similar to the Library. The walls of the hall are full of shelves holding various records. There are several groups of angels who are waiting at the different desks spread across the room. Angels appear to be writing official records, as the verbal reports are made by the ruling angels in charge. Angels move around the room like couriers with their rolls of parchment. As quickly as angels leave the room, more seem to arrive. I'm really impressed with the high level of organisation.

Thaniel explains, 'Serving God requires efficient use of resources by every angel. There's no room for failure, no shortage of personnel and no wastage. The work here is non-stop and it's a further reflection on the dynamic nature of God's eternal kingdom.'

I ask him, 'When Jesus taught his disciples to pray *"Your will be done on earth, as it is in heaven"* did he have Angel HQ in mind?

Thaniel smiles at my suggestion and says 'You know, I think he did. He certainly knew about it.'

I hear a distant blast of the piccolo trumpet behind us in the main commissioning chamber.

More tasks for angels in heaven, I think to myself, and I'm just a little curious as to what this latest call might be.

But there's no time! Another angel is talking with Thaniel, and I get the impression he's about to tell me something important.

'Jamie, we must go immediately to the Judah Gate!'

His voice sounds urgent, so I avoid asking questions. I know the Judah Gate is midway along the northern wall of the city. We arrive almost instantly and find ourselves walking in front of one of the grandstands close to the entrance. It's very noisy with lots of cheering and shouting, just like the moment when I first arrived at the Issachar Gate. We quickly find two empty seats not far from the front. Crowds of new arrivals are flooding into heaven. Above us, the angels are singing and there are constant welcome fanfares by the angel trumpeters, positioned with their backs toward us on the red jasper parapet.

I watch as the new citizens arrive. There are many older people, and a few people around my own age plus several little children. I see two children, a boy and a girl, walking hand in hand. They look so cute, and I wonder if they are brother and sister. Thaniel is also keeping a very close watch on the new arrivals.

Just as I'm peering toward the entrance I'm suddenly transfixed. I can't believe it. Tears begin to roll uncontrollably down my cheeks. It's my dad!

How could I ever forget his face? It's him, I just know it; he's wearing a white robe. Instinctively, I rush down the steps and make my way through the crowds knowing that at all costs I must keep him in sight. At last I reach him, throw my arms around him and kiss him on the cheeks.

'Dad!' is all I can say, as more tears flow down my face. We just stand there together, holding one another tightly.

Finally, with tears in his eyes and his voice breaking he speaks to me.

'Jamie, I knew you would be here.' He pauses. 'As I came out of the mist and approached the city gates I was convinced I would see you very soon.'

He asks, 'How did you know I was arriving?'

I look him in the eyes and say, 'Dad, it was the angel, it was Thaniel my guardian angel, he made sure I was here in time to meet you. Except he never told me it would be you - maybe he didn't even know.'

I tell him, 'Gramps and Grandma are here in the city and your brother, Uncle Frank. I see them regularly and we have wonderful times together. Oh Dad, there's so much I have to tell you. Heaven is a truly wonderful place.'

It dawns on me that my dad is older than I remember. He looks good, but he's definitely older. Dad gazes back at me.

He says, 'Jamie you haven't changed a bit. You look just like you did before you became ill. It really is terrific to see you.'

'Dad, how long is it since I died?' I casually ask.

He pauses to think and then replies, 'It's been twenty two years.'

I'm stunned!

'Twenty two years?' I repeat with utter amazement, as dad slowly nods his agreement.

174

I'm truly staggered to think I've been in heaven for so long. It feels more like just a few weeks. My time in heaven flashes across my mind. I see the many different places I've visited, all of the people I've met and the various things I've done.

We begin to walk together across the square; I suddenly remember Thaniel. I look across at the grandstand where we'd been sitting, but he's gone and is nowhere to be seen. Dad and I continue walking along Judah Street in the direction of the city centre.

'Dad, it's so good to see you again. Heaven is truly a wonderful place, beyond our hopes and dreams. I've made many new friends and everyone is so helpful and kind. The presence of the Lord is felt everywhere, but just wait until you meet Jesus in the Throne Room. He is just awesome.'

I feel very close to my dad right now. I'm surprised at how easily I can share conversation with him; there's no awkwardness. As son and father, I feel we are bonded together as never before.

'Jamie, I've missed you so much over these years,' Dad says. 'God gave your mum and me much comfort after your passing, and we all felt at peace after your funeral. We came to realise that God knows best, and that he must have a higher calling on your life. As a family we often talked about you; we remembered you growing up, going to school and getting your first job. Your brother, Josh is now the pastor of a church in Swindon and your sisters, Suzie and Sarah are both happily married. Many of the people in the church, who prayed for your healing while you were ill, became stronger in their faith. Some of your friends like Stuart and Steven went into full time Christian ministry. Your girlfriend, Catherine struggled at first to come to terms with your death, but eventually she met another young man and married him. She's now a primary school teacher in Cornwall and has two fine teenage sons.'

'Dad, that's so good to hear,' I respond.

I now understand God's ways more clearly and have learned that he has absolute power and is in perfect control. I've observed how God's kingdom is governed in heaven and also seen how the angels constantly fulfil his purposes both in heaven and on earth.

As we walk along the golden highway, I point out to Dad some of the features of the city. I show him the blue canals, which run alongside the avenues, and tell him about the river, the fountains and streams. I talk about the trees, the flowers and the grass and how they live forever. I explain about the city centre, the towns and villages of heaven. Then I try to describe some of the special places I love to visit; the Throne Room, Praise Pavilion, the Library, the University, the Hall of Honours and the Banqueting Hall.

Passing close to the city centre, I show my dad several of the major landmarks, clearly visible in the brilliant light around us. We see the white dome of the Observatory nearby, and I then point out the much larger golden dome of the Throne Room.

'Jamie, did I hear you mention Gramps and Grandma?' Dad asks.

'Yes, of course, let's go and see them,' I respond. 'They will be so pleased to see you.'

Making our way along Issachar Street, we cross Rachel Avenue and the canal, and soon reach the courtyard beside their apartments. Perfect timing. Sitting on a bench in front of the small fountain are Gramps, Grandma Minnie and two other ladies, with their backs to us.

'Gramps,' I call out.

All four look up to see me and dad arriving.

'Edward, it's you!' they call out to Dad, clearly overjoyed, and with their eyes fixed on him. Immediately I recognise my two great aunts.

My dad calls out, 'Mum, Dad, Annie and Alma'.

They all stand up and move quickly towards us, with arms outstretched. We all embrace and kiss each other with tears of joy and laughter.

My dad then turns to me, 'Jamie, do you remember your great aunties, Annie and Alma?'

'Of course,' I reply, 'especially the time we all went on the Easter egg hunt at Henley on Thames.'

Annie and Alma chuckle to themselves.

'What a wonderful reunion,' says Grandma, wiping the tears from her cheeks with the back of her hand.

'Jamie, how did you find your dad?' Gramps asks.

'Oh, that was all down to Thaniel. We were visiting Angel Headquarters when he got the call to take me straightaway to the Judah Gate. We got there just in time for me to see Dad coming through the entrance. I'm so glad I spotted him among all those people.'

Just then my Uncle Frank returns from the Library and recognises his brother standing with us.

'Eddie, is that you?' he calls out.

Dad responds, 'Frank, it's wonderful to see you again,' and he holds him in his arms. Sight of her two sons reunited in heaven brings more tears of joy to Grandma Minnie and her sisters.

All of us sit down on adjacent benches. We listen to Dad with great interest as he shares his news with us. The family members tell him about their wonderful times in heaven and all the joy they have. The conversation lasts a long time, as the water from the crystal fountain splashes and bubbles with life.

Eventually, we all walk with Dad to his own apartment, very close to mine. My grandparents, uncle and aunts say their goodbyes. Dad and I get some time alone, relaxing on the sofas and taking in the city views. I share with him about my experiences of heaven. He really likes the idea of heaven's special buildings appearing like jewels in the royal crown - as explained to me by Gramps. This naturally appeals to his love and fascination with gemstones.

I talk for a long time about the Throne Room, of God's appearance and the wonderful sight of Jesus Messiah. I tell him about the angels, the cherubim and the seraphim. He also hears about the archangels and the twenty-four elders.

I ask, 'Dad, are you ready to go to the Throne Room with me?'

He smiles at me and says with a twinkle in his eye, 'The Throne Room? Where else would I rather go? Of course I can't wait to meet the Lord.'

AS IT IS IN HEAVEN

The reunion with my dad has had a great impact on my life in heaven. It was thrilling and also humbling to have the opportunity to be there at the gates, the very moment he arrived. I'm hugely thankful to my heavenly Father, who arranges everything in his perfect timing. For Gramps and Grandma to see their other son again makes their lives all the richer.

My close friends, Pieter, Ishran and Hannah, have each talked with me about their own hopes of being reunited with members of their own families. It's mind-blowing to realise that when we meet our loved ones again, in this city - it's forever!

There's certainly no burden of grief in heaven. This is because the great love of God dispels all anxiety and concern about those we love on earth. Heaven is a realm where hope is fulfilled; it's a place of laughter, with plenty of fun, and a city of great joy.

I'm taking my dad on his first visit to the Throne Room. I reckon he's well prepared for what's in store. Or so I think! But, before we go there, I've a special reason to call in at the Library.

We leave his apartment and make our way along the pathways to Rachel Avenue. Dad is looking really well and appears to be much more relaxed, than when we first met at the gates. I've noticed that his face really shines and his smooth skin has no wrinkles. It's wonderful to peer again into his brown eyes and see his sparkle of humour and wit. In many ways, my dad looks much like his mother, Grandma Minnie.

As we walk along the canal, I tell my dad about the river, which flows from God's throne along the middle of Benjamin Street. He laughs out loud, when I tell him about the time I went for a swim in the river with my guardian angel. I tell him about how I met Ishran, in one of the many gardens, and how we've become such great friends.

We make our way down Issachar Street and pass Miriam Avenue, before stopping to sit down on one of the crystal benches in Fountain Square. The tall buildings of the city centre all around us are as breath-taking as ever; especially the gleaming, gold dome of the Throne Room. I also point out the attractive, white mansard roof of the Library not far away.

Just then, I see Thaniel walking straight toward us with another angel who I don't recognise.

'Jamie!' Thaniel calls out, 'I was hoping to see you.'

Dad and I both stand up.

'Thaniel,' I say, with a brief glance toward Dad. 'I'd like you to meet my dad, he's called Edward. I think you knew he was arriving. Thank you so much for bringing me to the Judah Gate; we got there just in time.'

'Dad, please meet Thaniel, he's my favourite angel. The one I've told you so much about.'

Thaniel puts his strong arms around my dad.

He says, 'Welcome to heaven, Edward. You have a wonderful son. Jamie and I are such great friends.'

He continues, 'Edward, I'd like you to meet my friend Zelah. He knows you very well and that's because he is your guardian angel.'

Zelah is slightly taller than Thaniel with a full head of white hair and a shining robe; he appears confident and outgoing. At this moment, I expected Dad to shake his hand in his customary British manner, but oh no! Dad throws his arms around Zelah, as if he was a long lost friend.

Dad says, with emotion in his voice, 'How wonderful to meet you Zelah. There have been several times when I sensed you close to me while on earth. But now I get to meet you in person.'

180

Zelah gives dad a big smile and says, 'I know we'll both have great times together here in heaven.'

Thaniel then explains that Zelah and himself are on their way to the Hall of Honours, to witness the next ceremony, so they need to leave us. We say our goodbyes.

We leave the square with its trees and fountain, and after a short distance reach the front of the Library. Dad admires the emerald-green walls and carved entrance steps, which lead up to the large rectangular building. I point out the viewing balconies built into the upper floor, from where we are being observed by several visitors.

Dad asks, 'Jamie, why are you going to the Library?'

I reply, 'I want to read one of the special scrolls before we go into the Throne Room.'

He asks me, 'Which scroll do you have in mind?'

'It's the Gospel of Matthew,' I answer and then add, 'I know where it is, so this shouldn't take long.'

We enter the Library together and walk along the passage into the great hall with its sea-green crystal floor. The scene is as busy as always, with scores of citizens criss-crossing the concourse and moving along the upper galleries. Among the crowds are numerous angels, with many carrying scrolls.

I wonder to myself, how long will it be before the archangel arrives from the Throne Room to collect one of the sealed scrolls?

I show my dad a seat, near one of the many large alcove bookcases.

'Dad, you wait here and I'll be back very soon.' I tell him gently.

'OK, Jamie, I'll see you shortly,' Dad replies as he sits down.

I disappear through one of the archways and climb the red and white striped onyx stairs, as far as the second floor. Walking quickly along the gallery, I peer down at the concourse and smile to myself; my dad is sat just where I left him. It was only at our incredible reunion that I appreciated just how much I'd missed him, since my arrival in heaven.

Reaching the Treasury Room, I make my way over to the precious Gospel scrolls stored horizontally on shelves. Carefully checking the small labels hanging from the roll ends, I soon find the Gospel of Matthew. At that moment an attendant angel appears beside me.

He says, 'Let me open the scroll for you.'

'Thank you so much,' I answer, as he lifts out the scroll and lays it out with precision on the wide table nearby. I unroll the scroll with one hand, while keeping a tight hold of the golden rod and soon find what I'm looking for. I read the words aloud.

'Your kingdom come, your will be done on earth, as it is in heaven'.

The sentence is part of the Lord's Prayer, as taught by Jesus, in his famous Sermon on the Mount. Ever since my meeting with Jesus on the hillside, these words have been running through my mind. By reading out the words aloud, directly from the sacred Scriptures, I hope to gain a deeper understanding.

Once again, I slowly repeat the verse, 'Your kingdom come, your will be done on earth, as it is in heaven.'

Without any prompting, the attendant angel standing next to me quietly echoes the same phrase.

He whispers, 'On earth as it is heaven.'

Instantly the truth dawns on me, like a flash of revelation.

'Of course,' I say under my breath. 'On earth as it is in heaven.'

I thank the angel for helping me and make my way down the busy stairway to the Library's concourse.

I understand this little phrase in a whole new way. It seems to sum up so much of God's universal purpose. God's great desire is for his kingdom to be demonstrated *on earth as it is in heaven*. The church is called to model this life from above, until it becomes a reality for each community on planet earth. God chose the earth as his special dwelling place.

I think about the earth as the centrepiece of creation, with its moon, sun, solar system, galaxy and billions of stars.

I ask myself, did God use the pattern of the eternal heaven to create a time-bound universe?

Humans are made in the image of God; we all share a heavenly likeness. Are we really so different from the angels?

It all starts to make more sense. Abraham foresaw that God's kingdom would be established; on earth as it is in heaven. He knew that heaven was always the pattern. Eternity is the starting point as well as the conclusion. During his long journey of pilgrimage and service for God, Abraham the patriarch and father of all who live by faith, was inspired by this vision. He was fully persuaded that his family's destination was the heavenly city, whose builder and maker was God.

Arriving back in the Library's great hall, I notice my dad is talking to someone who's sitting next to him. Dad looks up and sees me approaching, and then I recognise who the stranger is.

'Lucas, this is my dad!' I call out with surprise.

Lucas replies, 'Yes, I know. Your dad has been telling me about how you met him at the gates.'

I tell my dad, 'Lucas is one of my special friends in heaven I told you about. He's the author of Luke's Gospel and the Acts of the Apostles. He's never far away from the Library and seems to know every inch of the place.'

Lucas turns to Dad with a smile and says, 'Edward, I'd be very happy to show you round sometime.'

Dad replies, 'Lucas that would be great.'

We both say goodbye to Lucas and leave the Library.

I'm keen to get to the Throne Room. As we walk along Issachar Street towards Throne Square, I tell Dad about my reading of the Gospel of Matthew scroll. He listens carefully as I share with him my latest thoughts about the patterns of heaven.

Arriving in Throne Square, we stop beside the steps, to take in the view of the magnificent Throne Room, across the vast blue plaza. Brilliant light floods out from its massive, golden-crystal dome and radiates through its translucent, yellow walls.

Angels fill the sky overhead. I point out, to Dad, the narrow circular balcony high up in the windowless wall, where the angels come and go. Scores of them are waiting for their turn to enter the holy place, through the hundreds of little openings. I'm reminded again of what Gramps said about the royal crown of the city. From high in the sky the dome of the Throne Room appears like a golden-yellow gemstone, set in sapphire. Dad and I stand together at the centre of God's diadem of delight, encircled by the colourful gems of the other great places that make up his crown.

We cross the crystal plaza and pass a cluster of trees covered in white blossom. Short bursts of water spring up from the ground like fountains, but as we try to dodge between the random spurts, our best efforts are in vain. Looking at each other, we both laugh as the light spray splashes our faces, arms and feet. At the entrance to the great Throne Room we become silent and prepare to go in. The towering walls are so high that we can no longer see the great dome above.

As Dad and I pass through the richly-jewelled western entrance, we begin to hear the muffled sound of song from deep within. Walking side by side we enter the most holy place, God's eternal home and the great throne of his kingdom. The singing echoes around us as we make our way down the long flight of shallow steps. On reaching the floor of the arena, large numbers of worshippers fill the cavernous room and occupy the tiers up to the angel balcony.

I'm learning that worship in the Throne Room never ends. Once the exclusive domain of angels, overwhelming numbers of citizens now join them, to meet with God and to offer their praise and adoration.

I ask myself the question, 'Should not the worship of the church on earth be the same as it is in heaven?'

A rush of holy awe greets us like a surging wave. The Throne Room is transformed into an ocean of God's love and power, as we step into its waters. I manage to exchange a brief smile with my dad, wanting to reassure him on his very first visit. He nods back and I know he's ok. The powerful presence of God seeks to draw us to himself. Do I let myself go in the current of his love or do I hesitate and wait?

I recall a similar moment, when on holiday with some friends at Watergate Bay in Cornwall. I stood hesitant in the shallow sea, wearing my wetsuit, with my board held close to my chest. I was waiting for the next wave to approach. As soon as it came I felt its powerful current. Immediately, I launched myself forward, pushing through the incoming wave to paddle my board out into deeper water.

Both Dad and I continue to edge forward along the floor of the vast arena, which spans more than 300 metres. The clear blue crystal beneath our feet appears like an ocean floor. Countless other eager worshippers are all around us and it's not long before we become separated. Although I'm glad that my dad is still in sight.

In front of us is Almighty God seated on his great throne and surrounded by the huge emerald rainbow. The glory of his presence shines with brilliance, as the cherubim gather tightly around the base of his throne and the seraphim hover overhead. This time my fear has gone and I move forward with eyes wide open. I don't want to miss anything; my heart and mind are ready to yield to the full measure of God's presence. My greatest desire is to be filled with God's glory.

The remarkable encounters that I've experienced in heaven flash through my mind; each one has been liberating. By spending time in different places I've discovered so much more about heaven and the realities of God's kingdom and already gained a deeper understanding of God's ways.

In Praise Pavilion, I saw worship expressed with creativity, colour and movement. I listened to the perfect harmonies of instruments and voices bringing praise to God. While in the arena, I also witnessed the collaboration between citizens and angels in honouring Jesus Messiah as Lord. My own heart melted like wax in his presence and I was transformed.

The time I spent in the rooms of the Library gave me many fresh insights. I understood why God inspired authors like Moses, David, Isaiah and the Gospel writers; each of them was on a unique journey of discovery. Their task was to write down a record of the things God did among his people; what he said and showed them. I've also glimpsed some of God's records about the way we live our lives and the things we say and do. Every one of us is accountable to God.

The scenes I witnessed in the Observatory also left a lasting impression and as a demonstration of God's love for the world. To witness the sending out of angels to assist believers in times of trial was truly remarkable. I also shuddered at the prospect of the terrible judgements that will come upon the earth one day, when the martyrs and suffering servants of God are finally vindicated.

The order and discipline I saw at Angel Headquarters showed the effectiveness of God's authority. This new perspective about the role of angels in the kingdom of heaven gave me much assurance about God's ultimate purposes for the church.

My visit to the University helped me to see firsthand how we continue to grow in our knowledge of God. I'm thrilled to discover we all learn new things in heaven. The limits of our comprehension of God and his kingdom are removed. In eternity we gain a full understanding of divine mysteries. It was also wonderful to see the men and women of faith continuing to teach the truth about God and his purposes.

My invitation to the Hall of Honours helped me place all service for God in its true context. There were actions I took on earth that carried eternal value and brought great reward. Just as there were activities I spent my time on that achieved no heavenly benefit. There were words spoken that were judged worthy of God's kingdom and other words that are not. Time on earth was finite.

My own life appeared to have been cut very short. How much greater is my life here in eternity, where there is no more fear of death. Even so, it was vital for me to choose God's way of truth and to believe in Messiah Jesus in order to enjoy eternal life. The consequences of an eternal hell and judgement are totally unimaginable.

The delightful celebration at the Banqueting Hall with the Lord and among those who are closest to me was an unforgettable experience. To sit at the Lord's banquet, to drink of the wine, and taste the food in his presence filled me with absolute joy.

I now stand before God's throne as one of his many sons, made worthy to fully share the glory and honour of Jesus Messiah. Finally, I understand what it means for Jamie Ocklestone to sit with Messiah at God's right hand. Messiah is the head of the church, his body on earth, as it is in heaven. The fullness of life I now enjoy in heaven is the same life poured out on people across the earth. I received the gift of eternal life when I first became a Christian. Just as the river of God flows from the throne and throughout heaven, so this living water is poured out from above to thirsty hearts on the earth. A taste of what lies ahead in eternity.

Somehow I'm drawn deeper forward towards the throne. In the surging swell I'm being consumed by each wave of divine power. Just ahead of me, I see the archangels standing side by side, ready to serve God and to obey his command. In these moments, worship is personal; it's between me and the Lord.

With barely a blink, I stand transfixed by the throne of God as it blazes like the sun. I begin to imagine one particular event, which took place long ago at this very spot. It was the time when Jesus Messiah returned to heaven, after his sacrificial life of service on earth. The gates of heaven were opened wide and the first citizens followed him in. Jesus came to this throne and accepted his rightful place at his Father's side. He was given a name of glory and honour, a name above every other name, that at the name of Jesus every knee would bow. Everyone will confess him as Lord.

Here in the Throne Room, God also gave to his Son the gift of the Holy Spirit, to empower the church on earth. Having received this gift, Jesus poured it out upon his church on the Day of Pentecost. It's the Holy Spirit himself who now brings the dynamic of the kingdom of heaven to believers on earth. I hear another echo of those words, *'Your kingdom come, your will be done on earth, as it is in heaven.'*

My eyes turn to Jesus as he stands glorified and I worship him. I think of the times I've seen him appear in the special places of heaven. In the pavilion, where he receives praise from huge crowds of citizens. From his royal balcony, he is presented with beautiful performances of dance, music and song. There too he is offered the crowns of those he has honoured.

This same Jesus, who stands in the Hall of Honours and personally rewards all who are faithful with crowns and commendations. Jesus Messiah, who joins his guests in the Banqueting Hall for a feast of food and friendship. Jesus, who also walks the streets of this city, who visits the homes of citizens, and sometimes sits down with the children in the village squares. How could I ever forget the time he came to meet me in the hills, when he spoke to me about his purposes in my life. My service for God in heaven has barely begun.

I ask myself, 'How many more people will I meet? What other places are waiting to be discovered? Will it be long before my reunion with other family members and friends who are believers?'

This is God's home. This is his city; where God the Father, the Son and the Spirit belong. Jesus has also prepared a perfect place for each one of us. Heaven is the heart of God's kingdom, the place from where he rules. According to the prophecies confirmed by the apostle John, this great city along with every angel and citizen will ultimately be relocated to a restored earth.

Here in the Throne Room all sense of time is absent; here is eternity. There is no end, just the ebb and flow of God's powerful presence. There's no schedule, no plan, no routine. This is God's Throne Room.

An awesome stillness now fills the room, as the glory cloud around the throne grows brighter, diffusing the light through the haze. Tens of thousands of worshippers across the arena remain motionless; many stand, others kneel and some lie prostrate on the floor. Each one of the honourable elders is bowed low before God with their crowns laid down in front of them. There is no voice or song to accompany the sound of fluttering wings, as countless seraphim hover high above the misty

189

throne. The powerful presence of God overwhelms me and I know that forever he is the Lord God of heaven and earth.

The only visible activity is the changing colour within the emerald rainbow over the throne. Flashes of neon light mingle with glowing ripples of blue and gold. This illuminates the wings of the seraphim and the robes of the angels who now fill the upper dome. Almighty God is revealed as all-powerful, the God who is the Creator, Preserver and Governor of all things. The Lord who is ready to act at any time. His every spoken word is backed by divine power. His kingdom is an eternal kingdom.

I fall to my knees in adoration as the cloud of God's presence envelops me. The golden glowing mist descends upon us all like a sacred mantle of glory. Those around me appear as silhouettes set in gold. Staring forward, I see the burning flame of God's presence, the same holy flame observed by Moses and followed by the children of Israel in the desert. These tokens of fire were also witnessed on the Feast of Pentecost.

I'm enveloped in the cloud. God has invited me to share his glory, the same glory he has given his son Jesus. The faint sound of singing returns as high above us the angels begin to offer their praise. A thousand tenor voices commence their song of adoration, which is truly tender and barely audible. The melody seems to float within the cloud and reaches God upon his throne. The song slowly increases in volume and I begin to catch some of the words. It's the song of the Lamb!

At this moment, I feel prompted to look behind me. In the bright mist, I see the bowed head of my dad as he worships the Lord Jesus. I manage to shuffle myself backwards and kneel alongside him. The angel's song begins to echo in my heart. I start to join in with the heavenly choir, as the phrases are repeated over and over again.

'Hallelujah to the Lamb, glory to the Lamb, worship the Lamb.'

I become aware of other worshippers, hidden in the cloud, who are also singing. I can clearly hear the women singing. As I look toward my dad, he lifts his head and turns to me without speaking. He grabs my hand firmly and slowly we stand up, side by side. I place my arm across his shoulders and we both begin to sing.

'Hallelujah to the Lamb, glory to the Lamb, worship the Lamb.'

At that moment I remember the words of my friend Pieter, when he lectured in the University.

He said, 'The time will come when we shall stand together to sing the song of the Lamb before the throne of God.'

Soon we will all sing the song of the Lamb before God's throne.

13919701R00115

Printed in Poland
by Amazon Fulfillment
Poland Sp. z o.o., Wrocław